Spring

ali smith
Spring

PANTHEON BOOKS

NEW YORK

All rights reserved. Published in the United States by Pantheon Books, a division of Penguin Random House LLC, New York. Originally published in hardcover in Great Britain by Hamish Hamilton, an imprint of Penguin Books Ltd., a division of Penguin Random House Ltd., London, in 2019.

Pantheon Books and colophon are registered trademarks of Penguin Random House LLC.

Grateful acknowledgment is made for permission to reprint the following previously published material: Random House, an imprint and division of Penguin Random House LLC, for permission to reprint an excerpt from "The Tenth Elegy" from *Selected Poetry of Rainer Maria Rilke* by Rainer Maria Rilke, edited and translated by Stephen Mitchell. Translation copyright © 1982 by Stephen Mitchell. Reprinted by permission of Random House, an imprint and division of Penguin Random House LLC. All rights reserved. • The Society of Authors as the Literary Representative of the Estate of Katherine Mansfield, for permission to reprint extracts from Katherine Mansfield's letters from *The Collected Letters of Katherine Mansfield,* edited by Vincent O'Sullivan and Margaret Scott, 5 vols., published by Oxford University Press, 1984–2008 (especially vols. 4 and 5; 1996 and 2008). Reprinted by kind permission of the Society of Authors as the Literary Representative of the Estate of Katherine Mansfield.

Library of Congress Cataloging-in-Publication Data
Name: Smith, Ali, [date] author.
Title: Spring / Ali Smith.
Description: New York : Pantheon Books, 2019. Series: Seasonal quartet.
Identifiers: LCCN 2019005846. ISBN 9781101870778 (hardcover : alk. paper).
ISBN 9781101870785 (ebook).
Subjects: LCSH: Seasons—Fiction.
Classification: LCC PR6069.M4213 S67 2019 | DDC 823/.914--dc23 |
LC record available at lccn.loc.gov/2019005846

www.pantheonbooks.com

Artwork on rear endpaper: *Why cloud,* 2016, by Tacita Dean, spray chalk, gouache and charcoal pencil on slate (60.6 x 67.4 x 0.9 cm, unframed). Copyright © Tacita Dean, courtesy of the artist and Firth Street Gallery, London

Jacket image: *Summer, 1922* (detail), by Boris Mikhaylovich Kustodiev. Private collection. Heritage Images/Getty Images

Jacket design by Oliver Munday

Printed in the United States of America
First United States Edition
9 8 7 6 5 4 3 2 1

To keep in mind
my brother
Gordon Smith

and for
my brother
Andrew Smith

to keep in mind
my friend
Sarah Daniel

and for
o bloomiest!
Sarah Wood

He seems to be a stranger, but his present is
A withered branch that's only green at top.
The motto: *in hac spe vivo*.
William Shakespeare

But if the endlessly dead awakened a symbol in us,
perhaps they would point to the catkins hanging from the bare
branches of the hazel-trees, or
would evoke the raindrops that fall onto the dark earth in springtime. –
Rainer Maria Rilke / Stephen Mitchell

We must begin, which is the point.
After Trump, we must begin.
Alain Badiou

I am looking for signs of Spring already.
Katherine Mansfield

The year stretched like a child
and rubbed its eyes on light.
George Mackay Brown

1

Now what we don't want is Facts. What we want is bewilderment. What we want is repetition. What we want is repetition. What we want is people in power saying the truth is not the truth. What we want is elected members of parliament saying knife getting heated stuck in her front and twisted things like bring your own noose we want governing members of parliament in the house of commons shouting kill yourself at opposition members of parliament we want powerful people saying they want other powerful people chopped up in bags in my freezer we want muslim women a joke in a newspaper column we want the laugh we want the sound of that laugh behind them everywhere they go. We want the people we call foreign to feel foreign we need to make it clear they can't have rights unless we say so. What we want is outrage offence distraction. What we need is to say thinking is elite knowledge is elite what we need is people feeling left behind disenfranchised what we need is people feeling. What we need is panic we want subconscious panic we want conscious panic too. We need emotion we want righteousness we want anger. We need all that patriotic stuff. What we want is same old Scandal Of The Alcoholic Mothers Danger Of The Daily Aspirin but with more emergency Nein Nein Nein we need a hashtag #linedrawn we want Give Us What We Want Or We'll Walk we want fury we want outrage we want words at their most emotive antisemite is good nazi is great paedo will really do it perverted foreigner illegal we want gut reaction we want Age Test For 'Child Migrants' 98% Demand Ban New Migrants Gunships To Stop Migrants How Many More Can We Take Bolt Your Doors Hide Your Wives we want zero tolerance. We need news to be phone size. We need to bypass mainstream media. We need to look past the interviewer talk straight to camera. We need to send a very clear strong unmistakable message. We need newsfeed shock. We need more newsfeed shock come on quick next newsfeed shock pull the finger out we want torture images. We need to get to them we need them to think we can get to them get the word *lynching* to anyone not white.

We want rape threats death threats 24/7 to black/
female members of parliament no just women doing
anything public anyone doing anything public we
don't like we need How Dare She/How Dare
He/How Dare They. We need to suggest the
enemy within. We need enemies of the
people we want their judges called enemies of
the people we want their journalists called
enemies of the people we want the people we
decide to call enemies of the people called enemies
of the people we want to say loudly over and
over again on as many tv and radio shows as
possible how they're silencing us. We need to say
all the old stuff like it's new. We need news to be
what we say it is. We need words to mean what we
say they mean. We need to deny what we're saying
while we're saying it. We need it not to matter what
words mean. We need a good old slogan Britain
no England/America/Italy/France/
Germany/Hungary/Poland/Brazil/
[insert name of country] First. We need the dark
web money algorithms social media. We need to
say we're doing it for freedom of speech. We need
bots we need cliche we need to offer hope. We need
to say it's a new era the old era's dead their time's
over it's our time now. We need to smile a lot while
we say it we need to laugh on camera ha ha ha
thump man laughing his head off hear that factory
whistle at the end of the day that factory's dead

we're the new factory whistle we're what this country's needed all along we're what you need we're what you want.

What we want is need.

What we need is want.

That time again, is it? (Shrugs.)

None of it touches me. It's nothing but water and dust. You're nothing but bonedust and water. Good. More useful to me in the end.

I'm the child who's been buried in leaves. The leaves rot down: here I am.

Or picture a crocus in snow. See the ring of the thaw round the crocus? That's the door open into the earth. I'm the green in the bulb and the moment of split in the seed, the unfurl of the petal, the dabber of ends of the branches of trees with the green as if green is alight.

The plants that push up through the junk and the plastic, earlier, later, they're coming, regardless. The plants shift beneath you regardless, the people in sweatshops, the people out shopping, the people at desks in the light off their screens or scrolling their phones in the surgery waiting rooms, the protesters shouting, wherever, whatever the city or country, the light shifts, the flowers nod next to the corpseheap and next to the places you live and the places you drink yourselves stupid or happy or sad and the places you pray to your gods and the big supermarkets, the people on motorways speeding past verges and scrubland like nothing is happening. Everything is. The flowerheads open all over the flytip. The light shifts across your divides, round the people with passports, the people with money, the people with nothing, past sheds and canals and cathedrals, your airports, your graveyards, whatever you bury, whatever you dig up to call it your history or drill down to use up for money, the light shifts regardless.

The truth is a kind of regardless.

The winter's a nothing to me.

Do you think I don't know about power? You think I was born green?

I was.

Mess up my climate, I'll fuck with your lives. Your lives are a nothing to me. I'll yank daffodils out of the ground in December. I'll block up your front door in April with snow and blow down that tree so it cracks your roof open. I'll carpet your house with the river.

But I'll be the reason your own sap's reviving. I'll mainline the light to your veins.

8

What's under your road surface now?
What's under your house's foundations?
What's warping your doors?
What's giving your world the fresh colours?
What's the key to the song of the bird? What's
forming the beak in the egg?
What's sending the thinnest of green shoots
through that rock so the rock starts to split?

It is 11.09 on a Tuesday morning in October 2018 and Richard Lease, the TV and film director, a man most people will best remember for several, well, okay, a couple of, critically acclaimed Play for Today productions in the 1970s but also many other things over the years, I mean you're bound to have seen something he did if you've lived long enough, is standing on a train platform somewhere in the north of Scotland.

Why is he here?

That's the wrong kind of question. It implies there's a story. There's no story. He's had it with story. He is removing himself from story, more specifically from story concerning: Katherine Mansfield, Rainer Maria Rilke, a homeless woman he saw yesterday morning on a pavement outside the British Library, and over and above all of these, the death of his friend.

Scrap all the stuff above about him being a director you've heard of or not.

He's just a man at a station.

So far the station is at a standstill. Delays mean there've been no trains coming into or going out of this station, not for the time he's been standing on its platform, which is sort of like the station is meeting his needs.

There's no one else on the platform. There's no one on the platform opposite.

There will be people here somewhere, people who work in the office or look after the place. Surely people are still paid to look after places like this in person. There will be someone watching a screen somewhere. But he's seen no actual people. The only other person he's seen since he left the guest house and walked along the high street is someone moving about in the open hatch of one of those coffee trucks outside the station, one of those Citroën vans, someone serving no one.

Not that he is looking for anyone. He isn't, and nobody's looking for him, nobody that matters.

Where the fuck is Richard?

His mobile is in London, in a half-full coffee tumbler with its lid on in a waste bin in a Pret a Manger on the Euston Road.

Was. He has no idea where it'll be by now. Rubbish depot. Landfill.

Good.

Hi Richard, it's me, Martin Terp's due here any minute, can you give me an approximate arrival time for you? Hi, it's me again Richard, just to let you know Martin's just arrived at the office. Any chance you could give me a call and let me know when we can expect you? Richard, it's me, can you call me? Hi Richard, me again, I'm just trying to reschedule this morning's meeting given that Martin's only in London till tonight, he's not back in town till next week, so give me a call and let me know about this afternoon will you? Thanks Richard, I'd appreciate it. Hi Richard, in your absence I've rescheduled us for 4pm, can you confirm when you get this message that you got this message please?

No.

He is standing in the wind with his arms folded holding his jacket against him to stop it flapping (cold, no buttons, buttons lost) and looking at the little white flecks in the platform tarmac under his feet.

He takes a deep breath.

His lungs hurt at the top of his breath.

He looks to the mountains at the back of the town. They are really something. They are really bleak and true. They're everything that a mountain can mean.

He thinks of his own place in London. Dust particles will be hanging in the sun coming through the cracks in the blinds, if it's sunny in London right now.

Look at him, storying his own absence.

Storying his own dust.

Stop it. He's a man leaning on a pillar in a station. That's all.

It's a Victorian pillar. The pillar's ironwork is painted white and blue.

Then he steps back under the bit of see-through roof over the platform, goes a bit closer to the buildings to get out of the wind.

Some of those mountains over there have what looks like raincloud over their tops, like their tops are veiled. The cloud the other way, direction south he'd say, looks like a wall, a wall lit from behind. The cloud over the mountains, north, northeast, is mist.

It's why he'd got off the train here: the train had pulled towards this station and there'd been something clean about the mountains, clean like swept clean. They had something about them that accepted the fact of themselves, demanded nothing. They just were.

Sentimentalist.

Self-mythologizer.

The automaton voice above his head now apologizes again for the fact that no train is currently arriving at the station or leaving from the station.

Almost nothing is happening, give or take the automaton announcements, a few birds crossing the sky, the rustle of the early autumn leaves, the weeds and the grass in the wind.

A man standing at a station looks at the mountains all round him in the distance.

Today they look like a line drawn freehand by a huge hand then shaded in below, they look like something asleep and waiting. They look like the prehistoric backs of imagined sleeping sea-beasts.

Story of mountains.

Story of myself avoiding stories.

Story of myself getting off a fucking train.

He shakes his head.

He was a man on a railway platform. *There was no story.*

Except, there is. There always fucking is.

Why was he on a station platform? Was he waiting for a train?

No.

Was he going somewhere? For what reason? Was he meeting someone off a train?

No.

Then why was the man on the railway platform at all if it's not about getting or waiting for a train?

He just was, okay?

Why? And why are you using the past tense about yourself, you loser?

Loser, yes. That's fair. Something had been lost. Something is.

What is? What exactly?

Well, I don't know how to describe it.

Try.

(Sighs) I can't.

Try. Come on. You're supposed to be Mr Drama. What does it look like?

Okay. Okay, so, so imagine someone or something, some force or other, bearing down on you head first and going through you from head to foot with, with an apple-corer, so that you're still standing there as if nothing's happened whereas actually something *has*, what's happened is you're a hollow man, there's a hole all through you where the core of you once was. Will that do?

Self-indulger. Dross. Tom and Jerry cartoon self. What, you want sympathy for your own hollowness? your, what? lost fucking *fruitfulness*?

Look, I'm just trying to put what I'm feeling into words, a feeling that's not easy to describe, into –

Don't story yourself to me, you waste of –

time in his life when he was able to love, literally be in love with, be at actual soul level happily infatuated with something like the simplicity of a lemon. Just any lemon, in a bowl, or on a market stall, or in a net with other lemons waiting to be bought at a supermarket. There was a time in his life when such a thing had filled him with joy.

But now it was as if such simplicity had, without him even noticing it happening, grown very small and far away and him on the deck of an old ocean liner heading towards rough sea and waving like a madman back at a shore which, like a time when there'd been a steady kind of joy in something like the simplicity of a lemon, had disappeared, vanished completely, was no longer visible to the eye.

Is no longer.

Loser.

When he thinks about the first time he met Paddy, what comes into his head is a black and white image from near fifty years ago of some teethmarks in a piece of chocolate, a piece grown so old already by the time he saw it that it had literally whitened, especially at the place where the impress of the row of little teeth was. The teeth were Beatrix Potter's. Beatrix Potter had at some point taken a bite out of the chocolate then put it down and forgotten about it in the shed where she wrote and illustrated the books about the charming English animals wearing the Edwardian clothes and being good and bad and stupid, the duck flattered by the fox, the squirrel who eats so many nuts he can't get out of the hole in the tree trunk; she had bitten into a pre-war chocolate bar and the impress of her teeth had outlived her, there in the hut, for decades after her death in 19-whatever.

He'd been assistant to one of the assistant directors, one of his earliest jobs. It was the first one he worked on scripted by Paddy.

Her script had turned a mostly uninspired shoot into a thoughtful film. More, she'd written the shots about the teeth in the chocolate into the script, so in the end they had to use the shots.

He'd got her address off someone and contacted her when they offered him his first solo. He'd bought her a whisky in the Hanged Man. He'd just turned twenty one. He'd never bought anyone a whisky in a pub before, let alone a woman, let alone a glamorous older woman like her.

— *Because I'm Irish?*

— *Because you're good.*

— *As it happens, I am, you've got that dead right. I'm very very good at what I do. Now, what about you, are you good? I only want to work with the very good.*

— *I don't know yet. Probably not. I'm more the self-serving type. But you got it, the teeth in the chocolate. You wrote it in.*

— *Yeah, you've a good eye. I'll give you that. And you're very young. So a lot's still possible. And you want me to work with you so much because I wrote something into it that meant they had to use your shots. Is that it?*

– Truthfully? It's your script that got me this job.
(She shakes her head, looks away towards the pub door.)
– But also, you made that film better. Your script made something real happen.
– Real, is it?
(Pause. Cigarette, inbreath, outbreath smoke.)
– Okay.
– Okay? Really? You will?
– Okay, I'll work with you. Play for Today, is it? Okay. On condition we do something more, something a bit more unexpected, in the slot.
– Unexpected how?
– There's ways to survive these times, Doubledick, and I think one way is the shape the telling takes.

Yesterday morning, a month to the day since the memorial service (they'd had her privately cremated some time before the memorial, he doesn't even know when, close family only), he is walking along the Euston Road and as he passes the British Library he sees a woman sitting against its wall, thirties, as young as twenties maybe, blankets, square of cardboard ripped off a box on which there are words asking for money.

No, not money. The words on it are please and help and me.

He's passed countless homeless people even just this morning coming through the city. Homeless people are that word countless again these days; any old lefty like him knows that this is what happens. Tories back in, people back on the streets.

But for some reason he sees her. The blankets are

filthy. The feet are bare on pavement. He hears her too. She is singing a song to nobody – no, not to nobody, to herself – in a voice of some notable sweetness, at a quarter to eight in the morning. It goes:

> *a thousand thousand people*
> *are running in the stre-eet*
> *oh nothing nothing nothing*
> *oh nothing nothing nothing*
> *oh nothing*

Richard keeps going. When he stops keeping going he is just past the front of King's Cross station. He turns and goes in, as if that's what he meant to do all along.

There is a stall in the middle of the concourse beneath the giant Remembrance poppy. The stall is selling chocolate in the shapes of domestic utensils and tools: hammers, screwdrivers, pliers, cutlery, cups and so on; you can buy a chocolate cup, a chocolate saucer, a chocolate teaspoon and even a chocolate stovetop espresso-machine (the stovetop machine is costly). The chocolate things are extraordinarily lifelike and the stall is thronged with people. A man in a suit is buying what looks like a real kitchen tap, made of silver-sprayed chocolate; the woman selling it to him places it delicately into a box she first lines with straw.

Richard puts his card into one of the ticket machines. He inserts the name of the place that's the furthest a train from here can go.

He gets on to a train.

He sits on it for half a day.

An hour or so before the train reaches this final destination he'll see some mountains against some sky through the window and he'll decide to get off the train at this place instead. What's to stop him doing what he likes, getting off at a place not printed on the ticket?

Oh nothing nothing nothing.

King Gussie, to rhyme with fussy, is how he'd always thought it was said, like the robot announcer pronounces it over the speakers in London King's Cross above his head before he boards the train.

Kin-*you*-see is how it's said by the guest house people whose door he knocks on when he gets there. They will be suspicious. What kind of person doesn't book ahead on his phone? What kind of person doesn't have a phone?

He will sit on the edge of the strange bed in the guest house. He will sit on the floor and brace himself between the bed and the wall.

By tomorrow his clothes will have taken on the air-freshener smell of the room he'll spend the night in.

11.29. An automaton voice apologizes over
the station speaker system that the 11.08 ScotRail
service from Edinburgh Waverley is delayed due to
a rail incident south of Kingussie, that the 11.09
ScotRail service to Inverness is delayed due to a
rail incident south of Kingussie, that the 11.35
ScotRail service from Inverness is delayed due to
signalling problems and that the 11.36 ScotRail
service to Edinburgh Waverley is delayed due to
signalling problems.

Virtue signalling problems, Richard tells his
imaginary daughter.

This calls for some serious no-platforming,
his imaginary daughter says.

(His imaginary daughter is still with him,
even if Paddy's dead.)

Whenever he's not sure what something

particularly current means, he asks his imaginary daughter. For instance, #metoo.

It means you're implicated, his imaginary daughter told him. You too.

Then she'd laughed.

What's a hashtag? he'd asked her.

She's been about eleven years old now in his head for a couple of decades. He knows it's patriarchal of him, wrong of him, not to have allowed her, so far anyway, an adult life. (He reckons he's probably not the only father, not by a long chalk, who feels like that or who'd do this if he could.)

A hashtag is quite different from a hash brown, his imaginary daughter said. Don't try to eat one. Or smoke one.

In honour of his real daughter, wherever she is in the world, presuming she's still in the world, he looked it up online to see what it really meant.

About time too, he thought when he did.

Then he didn't sleep for a fortnight, lying awake at 4am night after night worrying about this time or that when he'd thought it was all right to act however he liked to the women he was with. He'd touched many a leg. He'd taken many a chance. He'd been lucky more often than most. No one'd complained.

At least, not to him.

After a fortnight he started sleeping again. He was too tired not to.

I was sometimes a bit of a devil, you know, he'd told his imaginary daughter in his head.

I'd expect nothing less, his imaginary daughter said.

I was sometimes a bit of a devil, you know, he'd told his real daughter in his head.

Silence.

Last March. Five months before she will die. He navigates the miles of pavement slush between his place and hers. He rings the doorbell. One of the twins lets him in. Paddy is through the back. She hears him in the hall and starts shouting.

Is that my beloved king of the arts?

She's the kind of thin that looks like her arm might break if it lifts a mug of tea. But the spirit of her is full-force-gale at him as he comes through, about his hair being too long, his shirt stained from, what've you been doing, madman-eating? look at your trousers, have you no boots? look at your poor lovely shovelback chest in the terrible stained shirt, Dick, who do you think you are, bloody Pericles of Tyre?

Pericles of Tired, he says. Six miles through blizzards, to talk good governance with you.

Oh *you're* the tired one, are you, you self-indulgent fraudster. It's me that's the dying woman, she says. Take those wet shoes off.

You'll never die, Paddy, he says.

Oh yes I will, she says.

Oh no you won't, he says.

Grow up, she says, it's no pantomime, we all will, it's a modern fantasy and malaise that we won't, don't fall for it, and right now it's my turn for the boat with the hole in it, not yours, so back off.

We're all in that same boat, Pad, Richard says.

Stop thieving my tragedy, she says. Put the shoes on top of that radiator. Get the socks off your feet and up on to the radiator. Dermot, bring a towel and put the kettle on.

Ship of the liberal world, he says. We thought we'd be shipmates sailing that ship into the sunset horizon forever.

All changed, changed utterly, she says. How's the ship of the new world order shaping up out there, then?

He laughs.

Shape of a ship in a computer game, he says. Digitally designed to be torpedoed.

Human ingenuity, she says. You have to applaud it, finding such interesting new ways to enjoy the destroying of things. How're you doing, apart from the end of liberal capitalist democracy? I mean, it's nice to see you, but what do you want?

He tells her his news, that he's just found out he's been assigned Martin Terp's latest.

Terp? Oh Jesus Christ, she says.

I know, Richard says.

God help you, and that's help you're going to need, she says. Assigned for what? to do what?

He tells her about the novel about the two writers who happen by coincidence both to live in and around the same small Swiss town in 1922 but don't ever meet each other.

Katherine Mansfield? she says. Really? Are you sure?

That's the name, he says.

Neighbours with Rilke? she says. And is it true?

The acknowledgements page at the back of the novel swears it's true, he says.

What kind of a novel? she says. Written by whom?

Literary, he says. Second novel by Nella something, Bella. A lot of language. Not much happens.

And they've given a project like this to Twerp? she says.

It's a bestseller. Been on all the shortlists, he says.

I'm a bit off that particular radar, she says. Any good?

Paperback blurb says an idyll of peace and quiet, a gift from the past, be swept away, luxuriate, escape from an era of Brexit, all that, he says.

I quite liked it. Two people live quiet writerly lives and pass each other sometimes in a hotel corridor. One's finishing a life's work, though she doesn't know it. She's ill. To get away from fighting with her husband, who's further up the mountain, she's come down it to live in this hotel with her friend, a rather mousy-seeming character. The other writer, how do you say the name?

Rilke, Paddy says.

He's finished a life's work earlier that year, Richard says, he's exhausted. He's got renovations happening in the tower he lives in, so he's moved down the road into the same hotel till the renovation finishes. It finishes, he's off home, and he leaves the hotel just as she arrives, with her friend like a packhorse carrying all their bags on her back. But he likes to eat there, so he wanders down the road most evenings for dinner, it's a ski resort and it's summer so the place is empty, the hotel as well as the town, and sometimes the two writers end up sitting not far from each other in the same dining room. Sometimes they walk past each other in the hotel gardens, and the novel goes on at some length about the mountains above them and them below etc just, you know, living their lives with all that grandeur of the Alps as their backdrop.

And what happens? Paddy says.

I just told you the whole plot, he says.

34

Hmm, Paddy says.

A season changes, he says. They never meet. Horses, cloche hats and little waistcoats, high grass, flowers, meadows with cows in them, cows with bells round their necks. Costume drama.

She shakes her head.

But Terp, she says. Disaster. Can you get out of it?

He holds up the cuff of his shirt so she can see where it's frayed. Then he holds up the cuff on his other wrist, also frayed.

Have you seen any script? she says.

I have, he says.

Are there terrorists in it? she says.

They both laugh. Last year they'd watched together the whole iPlayer box set of National Trust, Martin Terp's latest drama, which has had rave reviews all across the media: five heaving-breast explosion-filled episodes about police and intelligence operatives dealing with a group of female Islamist terrorists who've barricaded themselves and some suicide vests into a north of England stately home with several members of the public and a newly qualified Historic England guide as their hostages.

I'm here today to tell you, Paddy. There's worse than terrorists, Richard says.

He tells her that Martin Terp has already handed in a series of draft sex scenes, about which the

people at the UK broadcaster who originally
commissioned the adaptation and the people at the
massive online retailer that's largely funding the
film have all been very enthusiastic.

Sex scenes? Paddy says.

He nods.

Between Katherine Mansfield and Rainer Maria
Rilke? she says. In, what did you say – 1922?

In his tower, in her hotel room, in various other
hotel beds including her friend's bed, there's a bit of
lesbian interest too, and – wait, I'm not finished – in
the hotel's gardens in a little grotto where a string
quartet usually plays, in the hotel corridor wrapped
in a curtain behind a pot plant, and in the hotel's
billiard room on the billiard table, the balls go
everywhere. Comedy fuck, he says.

Paddy laughs out loud.

I'm not laughing at the comedy fuck, she says.
I'm laughing because it's not just laughable, it's
impossible. For one thing, Mansfield had fully-
developed TB by 1922. She died of it at the start
of 1923.

I know, he says. I'm already sore here because of
her fully-developed TB.

He takes her too-thin hand and puts it on his
chest. She smiles at him, raises an eyebrow.

Fish are jumpin, Doubledick.

Somatize and the living is easy. Since they started
working together, since Sea of Troubles when he'd

literally turned a shade of what she called Irish green for the six weeks of the shoot and she'd diagnosed it as seasickness, Paddy's theory's been that when what he's making starts to happen in his own body then the outcome's charmed, the outcome will be good.

He grins, lets go of her hand.

Can't make anything good without you, he says.

I'd gainsay you there but I can't, can I, now you've told me it's Terp that's the new me, she says. And don't make me even more annoyed. This is one I'd give a lot to be doing with you. Katherine Mansfield. Jesus, a script about Katherine Mansfield. And Rilke. Literary giants, Mansfield and Rilke, same place, same time. Amazing.

If you give a damn, Richard says.

Oh, I give a damn all right, she says. The stories Mansfield wrote in Switzerland were her best. And him, about to finish the Elegies, write the Orpheus poems. Their two brilliances, going down into the dark to find the ways to talk about the life and the death. The seminal remakers of the forms they were using. There, in the same room at the same time. The very thought. It's mindblowing, if it's true, Dick. Really.

Take your word for it, he says.

She shakes her head.

Rilke, she says. And Mansfield.

Now Richard remembers; now the penny drops. Katherine Mansfield will be one of the many women writers Paddy's told him about all along, one of the writers she's been telling him about for decades and he's never listened about or done anything much about.

He tells her something he makes up on the spot, that he'd always imagined the Mansfield she's talked about over the years as rather Victorian, a thin spinstery sort of person, a bit prim and innocent.

Prim and innocent! Paddy says. Mansfield!

She laughs out loud.

Katherine Mansfield Park, she says.

Richard laughs too, though he doesn't really get why it's funny.

She was an adventurer all right, and in all the ways, Paddy says. Sexual adventurer, aesthetic adventurer, social adventurer. A real world-traveller. A life of all sorts of loves, very risqué for her time, I mean, she was fearless. Pregnant God knows how many times, always to the wrong people, got herself married to a virtual stranger so her child by someone else would be legit, then miscarried it. Is that in the book?

No, Richard says. Nothing like that.

Got herself behind the lines in the First World War, Paddy says, to spend a night with a French lover who was fighting. She showed the officials the

postcard her 'aunt' had sent her saying would she
please visit urgently. Sent by her soldier lover.
Signed it Marguerite Bombard. Bombardment of
daisies! She shocked into distaste all those people
who thought *they* were the social revolutionaries.
Made them seem suburban, Woolf, Bell, the
Bloomsburys. A New Zealand savage they thought
her, the little colonial. Oh, she was a pioneer all
right.

Paddy shakes her head.

But the weight of a blanket on her chest in her
bed was too heavy for Mansfield in the year 1922,
she says. Never mind sex. In 1922, sweet Jesus,
from what I know, she was so weak she could
hardly walk from a carriage to the door of a hotel.
And hotels were a bit iffy about the consumptive,
wouldn't let a coughing girl stay. Different in
Switzerland, maybe, where consumption tourism
was an industry.

An industry how? Richard says.

Good clean air, she says.

How come you know everything about
everything, Paddy? he says.

Please, Paddy says. Don't get at me for knowing.
I'm a dying species, I'm that thing nobody out there
thinks is relevant any more. Books. Knowledge.
Years of reading. All of which means? I *know* stuff.

That's why I'm here, he says.

Thought as much, she says.

She wedges herself against the edge of the table and pushes back her chair. She takes hold of the side of the table and stands herself up. She takes a moment because standing up has made her dizzy. She sees him tense and move as if to help her.

Don't, she says.

She looks towards the booklined hall.

I think the Rilke I had is long gone to the heaven of the Amnesty charity shop, she says. A man beautifully dead well before he was dead. Look at this bowl of roses, he said, and forget all the distracting things in the so-called real world. But there's only so many angels and roses, only so much death-as-a-means-of-expression-come-into-me-and-me-into-you-and-together-we'll-conquer-death-by-dying that a woman can take. Especially a dying woman. But I'm being unfair.

She walks herself over to the entrance to the hall. She balances herself against the wall, then against the books themselves, and moves along the shelf until she gets to the letters of the alphabet she wants.

Nope, no Rilke left, she says. Told you I was unfair. But I've plenty Mansfield for you.

She pulls out a book, opens it, leans it and herself against the other books and flicks through it. She claps the book shut and tucks it under her arm. She pulls another couple of books out. At this point Paddy is still strong enough to walk across a room with two or three hardback books held against her chest. She lets them fall on to the table in front of him. He reads what catches his eye where one of them's fallen open.

A storm rages while I write this dull letter. It sounds so splendid, I wish I were out in it.

Ha, he says.

Paddy smiles. Then she taps with a claw-finger a couple of times at the date at the top of the open page, where it says 1922. She gets back to her seat and lowers herself into it.

A good useful year for you, she says. Something like one in five of all the millions alive in the world in 1922 belong to?

She raises an eyebrow, waits to see what Richard will say. He says nothing. He has no idea what he's supposed to say.

British Empire, she says. And thinking my way round the world, doesn't Mussolini start muscling up around now? Is any of this in that novel?

You know me, he says. I might've missed it. I'm not the world's most attentive reader.

And closer to home, 1922, the killing of Michael Collins, she says.

Of course, Richard says trying to remember who Michael Collins is.

Think about it, Paddy says. Ireland in uproar. Brand new union. Brand new border. Brand new ancient Irish civil unrest. Don't tell me this isn't relevant all over again in its brand new same old way.

She closes her eyes.

And maybe also remind Terp about Wilson, she says. That'd please him, even more assassination. I mean Henry Wilson, you know who he was?

Uh, Richard says.

Light Brigade-ist, Boer War commander, First World War Chief of Imperial General Staff, staunch Irish Unionist, and when the Republicans kill him outside his house it pours the petrol on the already lit fuse, the fuse on the Irish Civil War. But you knew all that, no? What else? (Paddy is off, she's flying.) 1922. Year when everything that was anything in literature fractured. Fell to pieces. On Margate Sands.

Absolutely, he says blankly.

What I'm saying is, she says. All this on a plate, *and* a gift of a story. Real people in the same place by chance, and not knowing, not meeting. Passing each other so close. Inches. That's brilliant in itself. But one's lost a brother to the war machine, the other's nearly lost his mind to it. And what they write, it changes everything. They break the mould. They're the modern. The likes of Zola and Dickens pass the baton to the likes of Mansfield and Rilke, the two great homeless writers, the great outliers. She was New Zealand, he was, what was he, Austrian? Czech? Bohemian?

He sounded pretty bohemian in the book, Richard says.

Not that kind of bohemian, she says. Listen. British Empire, German Empire, grinding round against each other like two giant millstones, all the millions already dead, and they're about to grind the millions down all over again in the next war. It could be something, Doubledick. It could be really something. Tell Terp. Nostalgia for the empire's back big-time. You could use that.

I hear you, he says. Yes.

And behind it all, Paddy says. Everything that a mountain can mean.

How do you mean, what a mountain can mean? Richard says.

God help them there in their Swiss village, she says, and those great jagged shark teeth of God all round them like they're already on the tongue of a giant mouth. In Switzerland, the so-called neutral zone, and there in the air too, as airborne as Spanish flu, the spores of the next dose of imperial fascism.

Yes, Richard says. Right.

(Christ, he is thinking as he says it.

What'll the world do without her?

What am I going to do without her?)

And that's just the start, she is saying. There'll be more. There's much, much more. I'll have a think. I'll make some notes, shall I, Doubledick?

Richard fills with relief as physically as if someone has just turned on a warm showerhead somewhere inside him. He may well be leaking with relief. He looks down at his clothes to check he isn't. He isn't. He looks back up.

Thank you, he says. Paddy. You're the best.

But I can't do it all for you, she says.

No, no, I wouldn't expect you to, he says.

He winks at her. She stays impassive, grave-faced.

You and your wants, she says. You'd have me sending you story research from beyond the grave, afterlife essays, Rilke this, Mansfield that, and even then you'd complain about the handwriting.

Paddy, he says.

You'll need to do the thinking yourself, she says.

I'm useless, Pad, he says. *You* know that.

No, you've always been talented at the seeing of voice, she says.

Ha, he says.

(No wonder he loves her so much.)

But you'll need to get tough, she says. Tougher than you are. You'll need to be ready to tell Terp where to get off.

Make me those notes, Pad, he says.

You can always refer back to your old note pad, she says.

Old joke between them. They laugh like schoolchildren. The twin who let him in the front door earlier appears under the hall arch.

We think it'd be best if you maybe went, Richard, he says. Our mum's looking a bit tired.

Working title? Paddy says.

She says it as if the twin's not there. Richard ignores him too.

Same as the novel, he says. To persuade people it's an adaptation of something a lot of people bought so it must be good.

And what's the novel called? she says.

April, Richard says.

Ah, Paddy says. Of course. What a name for a book. April.

She closes her eyes. She suddenly does look very tired.

He pulls on one still-wet sock. He stands up without his shoes on, picks them up off the radiator and holds them by their backs.

She clenches a fist on the table.

The simple flowers of our spring are what I want to see again, she says.

Richard pulls one sodden shoe on. The cold against his foot makes him wince.

So *this* is what they mean when they say someone's got cold feet, he says.

Stay as long as you like, she says with her eyes still shut. Make yourself some lunch. Plenty in the fridge.

Will I make you something? Richard says.

Oh God no, she says. I can't eat anything.

We've already got it covered, thanks, Richard, the twin says.

She keeps her eyes shut. She waves her arm in the air above the table.

As long as you like, she says. And take those books with you when you go. Take all the volumes of the letters. There's more, under M. On the shelves.

I'm not taking your books, Paddy, he says. There's no way I'm taking your books.

It's not like I'll be needing them, she says. Take them.

Still 11.29.

Richard breathes in. It hurts.

That's Katherine Mansfield's fault.

He is just a little fearful that he'll also start to somatize the poet Rainer Maria Rilke's leukaemia.

The story goes that Rilke went out into the rose garden he'd cultivated round the turret and picked some roses, because a beautiful woman from Egypt had arrived to visit him there and he wanted to welcome her with them. But a thorn on one of the stems got him in the hand or the arm. The little wound it made didn't heal. His arm got infected. His other arm got swollen too. Then he died.

And he was a man who wrote a great many poems about roses – there's an irony in that, even

Richard can see that, though Rilke's actually not a poet Richard has much read, not one he'd heard of till this year. Now that he's perused a bit of Rilke online he'd have to say, if he was talking to Paddy, that he doesn't really get it. How *can* a tree grow inside an ear? There isn't room.

Rilke the man, though, sounds quite a charming little chancer, at least from the novel and the sites that Richard's perused, in that whenever a lady came to visit him, he would ceremoniously stand in front of that lady at some point in the visit and read her a poem, and then he'd equally ceremoniously present her before she left with the poem he'd read to her, copied out in his handwriting and dedicated to her, and she'd go away from that tower thinking he'd written the poem especially for her. In reality the poems had maybe been written years before, and after Rilke died several ladies were very disappointed to find he'd recycled old poems on them, sometimes the same poem to several women.

But charm certainly opened a lot of doors for him, and Rilke apparently wasn't rich by any means but, being a poet, needed a lot of looking-after by patrons and matrons (could you also say matrons, or was that unfeminist? Would women be offended?). He particularly liked staying as a guest of rich people in grand palazzos and castles. Who wouldn't?

But the rose thorn. The poems given to the ladies. The charm.

The story goes, etc.

It's this kind of thing that Richard's running away from, isn't it?

Richard feels suddenly nauseous.

He might well *be* sick.

(Is that a symptom of leukaemia?)

He looks around him for a bin. He doesn't want to throw up on such a well-kept platform.

In which case, his imaginary daughter says in his ear. You're probably not going to throw up. You can't think about whether it's okay or not to be sick in a place if you're really going to be it. And an ear is plenty big enough for a tree. A tree in the ear. A rose in the blood. Look where I live myself.

He checks the time again.

11.29.

Is that clock broken?

Is a single minute really this long?

Is the clock that's broken the one inside him?

He goes out of the station and walks around the space at the front of it looking for something real to take his mind off some of the other realities.

There's a tall stone structure over there, a war memorial maybe. He'll go over and read the names of the dead on its sides.

But there are no names of the dead on it.

It says, instead, in gold letters on a plaque set into its stone:

MACKENZIE FOUNTAIN

GIFTED TO HIS NATIVE TOWN
BY
PETER ALEXr CAMERON MACKENZIE
COUNT DE SERRA LARGO
OF TARLOGIE
AND OPENED BY
THE COUNTESS DE SERRA LARGO
21st JULY 1911

It's an old drinking fountain, one with no water in it.

He circles it a couple of times. He reads the sign again. How strange. Scotland meets Portugal, is it Portugal? or South America? He feels for his phone, to check.

No phone.

So he goes across to the coffee truck in front of the station.

Écossécoffee
Tak a cup o'
kindness yet

There's no one at the hatch. He knocks on the corrugated metal of the side.

50

A woman comes through by sliding herself like a caterpillar over the front seats and thumping head first on to the floor. She looks quite annoyed that she's had to when she stands up and appears at the hatch. She looks sleep-ruffled. She seems to be wearing a sleeping bag; she holds it up against her chest.

Yes? she says.

Busy today, he says.

She looks at him blankly.

Did I wake you? he says.

Are you insinuating I'm sleeping in this van? she says.

He blushes.

No, he says.

So, what can I do you for? she says.

She is not as young as he first thought. She is dark round the eyes, her face more lived-in, more used-looking. Fifty? She sees him placing her and gives him a sarky look.

I was wondering if you could direct me to a public library anywhere near here, he says. I'll bet you're relieved that water fountain isn't working. I bet it eats into your profits. The plaque on the side of it has interested me. I mean, what can Serra Largo ever have had to do with here?

The library's closed, the woman says.

Richard shakes his head, doleful face.

What a time we're living through, he says. What

kind of a culture is it that wants its people not to know? What kind of a culture wants some people to have less chance to access information and knowledge than the people who can afford to pay for it? It's like something out of a totalitarian sci-fi. It'd have made a good film back in the 70s, I was a bit of a filmmaker then. For my sins. I still am. But it's different days, now, oh, very. Nobody would've believed these days possible if we'd told them then what would be happening now. I mean, this is Ragnarok.

No. It's Kingussie, she says.

No, Richard says. I mean it's the end of the world. I mean the closure of the libraries.

It's not like *closed* closed, the woman says. It's closed on a Tuesday.

Oh, Richard says.

Open tomorrow, the woman says.

Ah, Richard says.

Anything else? the woman says.

No, no, Richard says. No, thank you. Unless –

The woman raises her eyebrows, waiting.

I don't suppose you've got such a thing as a lemon, he says.

A lemonade? the woman says.

No, a lemon, just an ordinary lemon, he says.

No, I'm sorry, we've nothing like that, the woman says.

Well, okay, I'll take that lemonade, then, he says.

No, we don't actually have any lemonade, the woman says. We don't stock lemonade.

Oh. Okay. Then I'll have an espresso, Richard says.

I'm sorry, I've no hot water on the van today, the woman says.

Ah. Well. An apple juice, have you got an apple juice? he says.

No, the woman says.

Right, Richard says. Then just a bottle of water, please.

The woman laughs.

Always makes me laugh, people wanting to buy bottled water in Scotland, she says.

Still, Richard says.

Always, the woman says.

Or sparkling if that's all you've got, he says.

Oh. We don't do water, the woman says.

Well, what've you got? he says.

We've actually not got any stock on the van today at all, the woman says.

Why are you open, then? he says.

He gestures to the hatch.

Fresh air, the woman says. Help yourself.

She's about to go.

Sublime, the mountains there, Richard says quick. But sublime on a human scale. Compared to, say, somewhere like Switzerland.

Well, I suppose, the woman says.

It must be nice living among mountains of the less awesomely sublime, more friendly type, he says.

Friendly? the woman says. You're easy fooled. The friendly Cairngorms. A million and one horrific ways to die up there.

Really? Richard says.

Exposure, storms, blizzards, the woman says. Wind tunnel that can blow you head over heels into snowdrift you'll never get out of. Sudden snowstorms, I mean any month of the year. Even the high summer. White-outs, avalanches. People getting lost when the weather suddenly changes. Mist coming down out of nowhere on days when it can be beautiful weather just a few miles away, I mean, people can be sunbathing at Loch Morlich and it can be frostbite and ice up there, and no shelter for miles mind you, no houses, no roads, the snow can fall very fast indeed, and it'll tire you out to be just trying to walk through deep snow, and up to your waist it can be. And in the spring, when there's the thaws, the thin-looking streams that seem like nothing can get very big and powerful, and there's also the danger of people putting their whole bodyweights on what they think is the ground but is really actually melty ice over very deep water, aye, there's been more than a few drownings that way, and the kind of wind can be blowing in April and May that actually pulls bushes and little trees up by the roots and flings them at you.

Gosh, Richard says.

The woman looks at him with wryness in her eyes.

Gosh, he says again.

Aye, the woman says. Beautiful, right enough.

Yes. Well. Thanks, he says.

He turns to go.

And it was for the horses, the woman says. For the cows. Local livestock.

I'm sorry? Richard says.

The MacKenzie Water Fountain, the woman says. People say the water used to shoot up out of it to quite a height.

Oh, Richard says. Right.

Right you are, the woman says. Cheers. All the best.

She manoeuvres herself, still in the sleeping bag, back into the front seat compartment of the van.

Richard stands for a bit in the empty car park. Then he goes back into the station.

11.37.

He goes through towards the platforms. He stands on the empty platform again.

He contemplates crossing the bridge and standing on the other side.

A bit of a filmmaker.

The sound of his own voice in his ears saying stuff disgusts him.

For my sins. The stuff he says disgusts him. *What does Serra Largo have to do with here?*

He breathes in. It hurts.

He breathes out. It hurts.

The next time a train comes through this station and stops here, he will slip down in the gap between it and the platform, place himself across these clean well-kept tracks next to the wheels and let the carriage he's got himself under put an end to him by the weight of its unstoppable going-forward.

Oh nothing nothing nothing.

The mountains rise like stilled waves above the man at the station and the houses of the town.

An obituary appears in the Guardian about a week after she dies. It's been written by one of the twins. Patricia Heal née Hardiman 20 September 1932–11 August 2018.

She'd once been called Patricia Hardiman. He had no idea.

They didn't think to call her Paddy, the name she used in the credits, and they listed only the two most well-known of the seventeen productions they'd made together: *Sea of Troubles (1971) and Andy Hoffnung (1972), two critically well-received and influential early experimental dramas shown in the BBC Play for Today TV slot; Sea of Troubles caught the first voicings of what would become the Northern Irish peace movement, and Andy Hoffnung was one of the earliest UK TV drama productions to take the first steps towards articulating what had happened to people three decades earlier in the Holocaust.*

Sea of Troubles: from Beatrix Potter to petrol bombs. Up until then there'd been almost nothing about Northern Ireland; Whicker had made a series just a few years before and it'd been almost completely unbroadcast. Too risky. For Sea of Troubles they'd made the camera move as the human eye moves among real people, via fragments of the life of the real places they lived and the everyday things they said, keeping them anonymous and protected by never filming their faces, filming instead the things around them as they talked, catching the ways they used their hands, the smoke rising from their cigarettes, the things there on their kitchen tables or mantelpieces: rosary, picture of a monarch on horseback, pattern on a table's Formica, illustration of a sailor on a packet of John Player's, ashtray full or empty, cup, saucer, kettle on a stove, scrubbed-clean ceramic sink, sweetpeas through a window growing up a trellis, hair in a curler under a headscarf, rust on the corrugated iron of a blockade, police truncheon hanging on a hook by a back door, old cloth pennant folded neatly and placed behind a brick in a farm outbuilding.

A soldier patted down the legs of a longhaired teenage boy in jeans and a shirt. A soldier waved a metal stick at a group of eight or nine women.

A child's legs crossed a road in the distance beyond barbed wire.

People spoke about it in parliament. People understood more from it than they knew from a thousand newspaper reports. It *foresaw Bloody Sunday*. (Though anyone with just one eye and half a brain could have *foreseen Bloody Sunday*, Paddy said the next year when a newspaper critic somewhere wrote that Sea of Troubles had.)

Her first experimental docudrama. One of the first ever of its kind. His first real anything. His first anything good. And Paddy, safe in heaven dead now, dead as Beatrix Potter'd been to them back then.

Andy Hoffnung: Paddy'd sat next to a man at a Beethoven concert at the Wigmore Hall some time in the late 1960s. An die Hoffnung, he said, and smiled at her. She'd thought it was his name, and told him hers, then she'd seen in the programme it was the title of one of the songs.

They'd gone out to dinner after. (They probably slept together.) He'd told her almost nothing about himself. Paddy, sharp as an arrowhead, had gathered a great deal. He was half German, half English. He'd been shafted by the worst of both. He'd lost a lot at the hands of both, family, friends, home, all gone, and so on. And yet the most hopeful man I've ever met, she said at the time. I don't mean naively. I mean profoundly. I realized, talking with him, that true hope's actually a matter of the absence of hope.

How can that be? Richard said.

(Richard was jealous.)

I don't know. But I came away from him hopeful myself, and that's really saying something in my world right now, Doubledick.

This Beethoven man had taken her hand in his in a club they'd gone to, as if to read her future, tell her fortune, but instead of doing it he'd acted out a scene he'd remembered from a Charlie Chaplin film he saw as a boy, where Chaplin takes a woman's hand and looks at the lines on her wrist or her hand to tell her how many children she'll have. He counts them. He says she'll have five. Then looks at the lines on his own, counts them, and it comes to twenty five, thirty, thirty five, more.

Then he did this silent laugh, she said, he was imitating Chaplin laughing like a child.

What's his name? Richard said (jealous). Did you sleep with him more than once? Was he any good? He said these latter things only inside his head. From then on, whenever she mentioned, even in passing, anything at all about Charlie fucking Chaplin, he knew she was thinking of, was alluding to – as if in secret, as if nobody would know she was doing it but her, with no idea that Richard knew exactly what she was doing – the An die Hoffnung man.

She'd written the script in four weeks. It was ingenious, told the story by not telling it. A wounded man wanders London with an open demeanour. That's pretty much it. Frost, fog. Nothing opens to him, though one way or another everything he touches opens. He sits in a kitchen and holds up a postcard. It's sent from someone in some camp or other in the war.

It's fine here, the actor playing Andy Hoffnung says to camera.

He is reading what it says on the postcard.

But then, see, he says, what she writes is, *but I wish I were with cousin Eury.* Eury was a code between us for hell. Eurydice, a dead soul. She's saying she'd rather be dead.

It's the only moment the war surfaces in the script. Everything else moves unsaid under the London pavements, the tooth-gaps in the streets where the houses were, the stone steps on the war memorials, the mud by the river, the Thames, shifty against its own sides, the high closed doors of the public art galleries at five o clock, the parked cars in the failing light, the market after the market's over, stalls gone, broken boxes and cabbage leaves all that's left. He kicks a gutter turnip the length of the street in the fall of the February dusk.

Heal née Hardiman.

Richard closes the paper and folds it.

Paddy bursts into his head like that first day through the doors of the Hanged Man. Oh. Oh, she was so glamorous. Older than him, a whole seventeen-year-old girl older, and pretty much any older woman would've been glamorous to a man in his twenties, but she was so much more so, being so self-contained, so uncategorizable, an uncategorizable sort from the start. (*There's no such thing as an uncategorizable sort,* she said when he told her this, *you can't categorize the uncategorizable, you chump.*) Look at her, smoking like she didn't even know she was holding a cigarette and leaning back or forward in that chair in her do-I-give-a-damn way till the moment she'd say, and she did it every time, exactly the right thing. Effortless. Like she knew exactly what to do with a story. Like she held down a marriage, a job, twins to bring up, and then, when her marriage came apart, it somehow just made her even more carefree. When his own marriage would fall to pieces at the back end of the 1980s and he'd fall to pieces with it, he'd spend a month on her couch. She'd help him sort the house out after his wife and child going. She'd help him sort himself out.

He'd never met a girl like her. Well, a woman. She wasn't just a girl.

(Was that an offensive thing to say nowadays? He'd no idea.)

62

He'd sat opposite her in the Hanged Man that
first time and wondered if they'd ever end up
sleeping together. (Nowadays was *that* an offensive
thing to think?) They had. It wasn't relevant. It was
the only irrelevant sex he'd ever had. They were
bigger than sex. The people he'd slept with over the
years, before Paddy, after Paddy, even the woman
he'd married, were here then gone, and there was
somehow still Paddy.

There's a difference between narrative strategy
and reality, but they're symbiotic, she said to him
one day in the 1970s.

He was round at her house. It was a light spring
night. They'd been listening to the news on the
radio in her kitchen. The Maguires had just been
sentenced. (They'd serve, between them, seventy
three years in prison before their convictions would
be quashed and those of them still alive would be
released.) The sentence Paddy had just uttered had
something to do with the sentencing of the
Maguires. But for the life of him he couldn't
imagine what she meant.

Between what? he said. They're what?

She'd started to laugh, it was the first time she'd
laughed for a long time, and she'd laughed so much
that he stopped being hurt and started laughing too
and they'd laughed into each other's arms. Afterwards
she'd said,

I like a good fuck as much as the next person,

Doubledick, and that was a very good fuck. Thanks.

April 1st, 1976.

Then nothing else of that sort. They'd got on with their work and their lives.

Last April. *The* last April. Four months before she will die. Though nobody knows that yet for sure, obviously.

What everybody knows today is that it's the hottest April day there's been since the year Richard was born. They are saying it on the radio and TV like it's unthinkably long ago, another era.

Well, it is.

He calls into a Maplin's to buy a memory stick. Maplin, the chain, is closing down soon. EVERYTHING MUST GO. The place looks plundered. He asks a man – his badge says he's the store manager – whether there are any memory sticks left. The man shakes his head. Just too late Richard notices the dark, the red rim round his eyes, a man who made good, reached store manager level and now it means nothing, has come to nothing in the end.

His life as he knows it is at an end and I'm asking him about a bloody memory stick. I'm a blunt instrument, Richard thinks as he leaves the ruined shop.

He walks along the pavement in the unnatural heat.

I'm so stupid, he tells Paddy when he arrives at her house. I'm a galumphing lout in the world.

Paddy is all bone structure now. Almost all her fury has burned off too; she's become philosophical about things she was still raging about just days ago.

She'd raged, just days ago, about the British government and Ireland.

It's possible that they know not what they do, she'd said. It's equally possible that they know exactly what they're doing. I won't forgive them, nobody who knows what it was like will. Messing with the ancient hatreds.

She'd raged about other things too.

Oh, I understand Brexit, she'd said. So many people angered into democracy for all the reasons. What I don't understand is Windrush. What I don't get, can't get my head round, is Grenfell. Windrush, Grenfell, they aren't footnotes in history. They're history.

The whole of history is footnotes, Pad, he said.

Common wealth, she said. What a lie. Why hasn't there been an outcry the size of this so-called United Kingdom? Those things would've brought down a government at any other time in my life. What's happened to all the good people of this country?

Compassion fatigue, Richard said.

Fuck compassion fatigue, she said. That's people walking about with dead souls.

Racism, Richard said. Legitimized. Legitimized division 24/7 on all the news and in all the papers, on so many screens, grace of the god of endless new beginnings, the god we call the internet.

I know people are divided, she said. People always were. But people weren't, and aren't, unfair. Even British racism used to give way when it came to unfairness.

You've lived a sheltered life, Richard said.

Make me laugh, she said. I'm Irish. I was Irish in the 1950s. I was Irish when being Irish in London was like being black *and* being a dog. I know the British people inside out. I was Irish in the 1970s. Remember?

I remember, he said. I'm old, like you.

A twin appeared.

Calm down, mum, the twin said. Richard. Please. Don't encourage her to talk about Donald Trump.

We're not talking about Trump, Richard said.

We absolutely bloody aren't, Paddy said. Let's

never do anything a demagogue narcissist might long for us to do.

Don't, please, Richard, the twin said. And don't talk about climate change or the rise of the right or the migrant crisis or Brexit or Windrush or Grenfell or the Irish border.

Are you joking? Richard said. There'll be nothing left to upset her with.

Don't be calling it migrant crisis, Paddy said. I've told you a million times. It's *people*. It's an individual person crossing the world against the odds. Multiplied by 60 million, all individual people, all crossing the world, against odds that worsen by the day. Migrant crisis. And you the son of a migrant.

Richard, the twin said as if his mother wasn't there. I mean it. If our mother continues to get worked up like this when you come, we're going to have to ask you not to come any more.

Over my dead fucking body, Paddy said.

It makes her so fretful, the twin said.

I'm not fretful, Paddy said.

After you've visited we can never get her to take her medication, the twin said fretfully.

Too bloody right they can't, Paddy said.

Her dead fucking body:

They had medicated her out of life.

But she was *old*, she was *ill*, it was *time for her to go*, she had *no real quality of life left*. The

Oramorph metamorph: one week she'd been all facts and wit and energy. The next, *what's that squeaking? my ears are all squeaks*. Then she couldn't follow a conversation, then her face, all worry, like something was missing, she couldn't think what.

Not that she ever stopped using words bigger than everybody in the room.

We'll have none of that psychopomposity here, she said on her deathbed.

Not that she ever stopped really being here, even in the delirium of the drip. *What they're all forgetting about Windrush is that it's a river, and a river more often than not'll grow from a source and lead to more rivers then to something the size of an ocean.*

Does she really need to be on that drip? Richard said to the twin.

The twin asked Richard to leave the room.

Then the twin told Richard to leave the room.

The other twin was sitting outside the shut door on a chair on the landing. He was staring at his feet, or the floorplanks. To get past him you'd have to be careful not to knock him downstairs.

Does she really need to be on that drip? Richard asked the other twin.

What can I do? he said. I've no say. I can't tell him what to do. I'm the youngest.

Youngest by four minutes, Richard said. And

you're a grown man. You're in your fifties, for God sake.

The twin stared at the planks. Richard passed him, not very carefully, and went back to the flat.

Ten days later in the Guardian he read:

Patricia Heal née Hardiman.

But that's in the future. Now it's still April.

He tells her about the man in Maplin's.

Everything must go, she repeats as if it's a line of poetry.

And me asking him about memory sticks, he says. I'm the clumsiest man alive.

Memory sticks, she says. There's a sentence for you. Well, it does and it doesn't. Memory, I mean. Depends on the Oramorph, which makes a lot of things sticky, and a lot of things stick to you. Mainly actual shit.

She laughs.

Why are they giving you it? Richard says. Are you in pain?

Not at all, she says.

I thought people only took it at the very end of things, Richard says. You're nowhere near that.

Thanks, she says.

The twin, already hovering in the hall, gets agitated.

Can you leave now, please, Richard, he says.

I only just got here, Dermot, Richard says.

Paddy looks at the twin.

70

A generation of children who've no idea they're going to die, she says.

Mum, the twin says.

Dying's a salutary thing, Dick, Paddy says. It's a gift. I look at Trump now, I see them all, the new world tyrants, all the leaders of the packs, the racists, the white supremacists, the new crusader rabblerousers holding forth, the thugs all across the world, and what I think is, all that too too solid flesh. It'll melt away, like snow in May.

She says it all still looking at the twin.

I'll be back in a minute with the spoon, mum, the twin says. Don't be long, Richard. She's very very tired today.

The twin disappears through to the kitchen.

Paddy turns to Richard.

They want me dead, she says.

She says it with no rancour.

It's what's supposed to happen next, she says. That's how the story goes. It's natural, Doubledick. Kids. I should thank God they're finally agreeing with each other about something.

She closes her eyes, opens them again.

Family, she says.

At least you had a family, Richard says.

Yes, she says. I did. But so did you.

One way or another, largely thanks to you, he says.

She shakes her head.

Truth be told, I wish mine'd been a bit more like yours, she says.

Ha, he says. Well. Crazy weather out there. You're missing nothing, Pad. One of the worst springs I can remember. Snow up to here just two weeks ago. Minus seven. And now this. Twenty nine degrees.

You're wrong, she says. One of the loveliest springs I've known. Plants couldn't wait to get going. All that cold. All this green.

**so if you could kindly email us at this address
by evening of Tuesday,** 18 September at the very
latest any good anecdotes/stories about our
mother's life that you would like us to include in
speeches that will be made on 21st we will do our
best to incorporate them thanks very much also
any old photos you might have please scan and
send to us we would appreciate it as unfortunately
we have lost a lot of old photos out of cloud storage
when our mother deleted them off a phone and
they deleted themselves from iCloud and so far
the originals have not turned up. Also please
forgive nature of group email but there is a lot to
organize as you will appreciate, vbw Dermot and
Patrick Heal.

What does vbw mean? he asks his imaginary
daughter.

It means very big wankers, his imaginary daughter says.

He presses reply.

Subject: Re: Patricia Heal Memorial.

He deletes the name and the word memorial and types in: *story of.*

But then he can't bring himself to write her name in the subject box next to the words story and of.

He clicks the cursor into the message space.

Subject: story of

Dear Dermot and Patrick,

Thank you for your email. It was your mother who was the writer not me, so forgive the infelicities of expression there will no doubt be in this 'story' I am sending you to try to express what she meant to me. There are of course literally close to a million stories I could send you, to illustrate what she meant, both to me and in the world. But here is just one. When my marriage broke up 30 years ago and my wife and child left the country and to all intents and purposes left my life I was very depressed and for quite some time. One day your mother suggested that I 'take' my child to see some theatre shows or films, or take her on holiday, or to see an art exhibition – which basically meant of course anything your mother had made up her mind that I myself should make the effort to go and see. I said, 'But how?' She said, 'Use your imagination. Take her to see things.

Believe me your child will be imagining you too wherever she is in the world. So meet each other imaginatively.' I laughed. 'I'm serious,' your mother said. 'Take her to see things. And tell her to send me a postcard whenever you do go to see things or places. Just so I know you've taken me seriously.' I thought your mother was being very kind, but that it was a rather silly idea. But to my surprise I found myself doing just that, 'taking' an imaginary daughter to things I'd never have gone to otherwise. Arcadia, Cats, all the big shows. I saw works by Leonardo at the Hayward, by Monet at the Royal Academy, modern art, Hockney, Moore, I saw too many Shakespeares, I visited the Dome show at the Millennium. I can't begin to count the number of films and shows I saw at cinemas and theatres and galleries and museums all over the world, and strange as it may seem and still does seem to me, I did none of it alone, thanks to the gift of your mother's imagination.

He reads it over.

He despises himself instantly for using the past tense meant. What she meant to me.

He changes it to the word means.

He despises himself for all the your mothers.

He despises himself most of all for reducing Paddy to an anecdote.

There isn't anything about it he doesn't despise.

He deletes it.

Gone.

He reads their email again.

He thinks about photos, lost in a cloud.

What's that poem about clouds that Paddy likes? Liked. It rhymes the word cenotaph with the word laugh.

He writes in the message space:

Dear Dermot and Patrick,

I'd like very much, if I may, to read in honour of Paddy at her memorial service that poem she always liked about the cloud. The whole poem might be too long but I could just read, say, a couple of its verses. Let me know. Thank you.

He adds, to humour himself, and to make his imaginary daughter laugh,

vbw,

Richard.

The last postcard he'd sent Paddy had been of clouds. He'd sent it from an exhibition at the Royal Academy in the summer. He'd gone to this because it was by an artist Paddy liked; Paddy had a book of hers full of people's lost photos, which this artist had found in fleamarkets or junkshops. The photos were sometimes really good, sometimes just run-of-the-mill, sometimes excruciatingly bad or blurred or taken at terrible angles, of people, places, cars, animals, trees, streets, concrete buildings, often of things you couldn't have imagined anyone ever thinking merited a photograph.

The artist had republished them in their own book paying them the kind of artistic attention that important photographs merit. This had made something almost magical happen to them. Whatever they'd meant to the people in them or the people who took them had disappeared. Freed from their old personal meanings, it was not just that they could be seen for themselves, but like they'd become ways to let someone looking at them see how the world really appears.

A woman in winter clothes collapsing in hilarity against a wall in the snow. A surly-looking man next to a fence on which a thick tree branch has broken, next to a wind-damaged tree with a ladder balanced against it. A woman with a parrot perched on her hand in a suburban back garden, two other women watching, one at a table, one in the window of the house behind. A dog standing in an arc of hosewater lit by sunlight. A large man and a small child both smiling at the camera, in a red pedalboat on a boating pond. A red butterfly open-winged resting in snow.

When he had seen this artist's name on the posters all round town – there were for some reason simultaneous exhibitions by her in major galleries all across London this summer – he'd decided he'd go to one, to surprise Paddy by knowing to do it without being told to.

He showed the ticket person his ticket (expensive).

He pushed the swing door open.

The gallery room he went into smelled brand new and was largely hung with pictures of clouds. They'd been done in white chalk on black slate.

But the thing that stopped him in his tracks in this room was that one whole wall, also chalk and slate, was a mountain picture so huge that the wall became mountain and the mountain became a kind of wall. There was an avalanche coming down the mountain picture towards anyone looking at it, an avalanche that had been stilled for just that moment so that whoever saw it had time to comprehend it.

Above the mountain peaks the sky was a black so dark it was like a new definition of blackness.

As he stood there, what he was looking at stopped being chalk on slate, stopped being a picture of mountain. It became something terrible, seen.

Fuck me, he said.

A young woman was standing next to him.

Fuck me too, she said.

Where can we run to? he said.

They'd both exchanged looks, laughed scared laughter, shaken their heads at each other.

But then he'd stepped back from the mountainscape and looked round that room again at the other things in it, and the pictures of clouds on the walls, done in the same materials as the mountain, had made something else happen, something he didn't realize till later, till he'd left the room, come out of the gallery and on to the street.

They'd made space to breathe possible, up against something breathtaking. After them, the real clouds above London looked different, like they were something you could read as breathing space. This made something happen too to the buildings below them, the traffic, the ways in which the roads intersected, the ways in which people were passing each other in the street, all of it part of a structure that didn't know it was a structure, but was one all the same.

He'd sat on the steps at the back entrance to the gallery and turned over a postcard of the mountain. Tacita Dean The Montafon Letter, 2017 Chalk on blackboard, 366 x 732cm. He held it in his hand – like you *could* ever hold the size of that image in your hand! – and drew a ring around the measurement figures with his pen so Paddy'd get some idea. He addressed it to Paddy's house. *Everything that a mountain can mean*, he wrote above the artist's name. *Having a lovely time. Wish you were here.*

Then he'd changed his mind.

He tucked the mountain postcard into his back pocket.

He addressed instead the longest largest

postcard he'd bought, the one of three connected but separate pictures of an increasing cloud mass. On this card the pictures worked together like moving film frames and at the same time like stills, like windows. She'd like this one. Tacita Dean Bless our Europe (Triptych), 2018 Spray chalk, gouache and charcoal pencil on slates 122 x 151.5cm; 122 x 160.5cm; 122 x 151.5cm. *Dear Paddy. A message from the clouds. Having a lovely time. Wish you were here.*

He put two first-class stamps on so as not to underpay and jogged round to the post office off Piccadilly so it'd catch the last post and be there tomorrow.

He sits at the table now in his back room.

September.

Paddy is rubble and ash.

He looks at the message he just sent. It still says *story of* in the subject box.

(My favourite of all the postcards is this one, Paddy'd said to him one day a couple of years ago holding up an image of a bridge in Rome.

Oh, that one, he said. Yes. I remember.

She read out what he'd written on the back.

Dear Paddy, my father is in tears because the old man who usually plays the saxophone on this bridge, with the little home-made canopy over his head fixed to his shoulders like an extra instrument in a one-man-band kit, like shade has to be part of

*the orchestra, one of the instruments, in a hot
country, has disappeared this year, canopy and all,
and a much younger different man is playing funky
guitar through an amp in his place instead. Or
some days nobody there playing anything at all.
My father is a sentimental old fool. But you know
this already. Every day he makes me come back
and check this bridge to see if the saxophone man
is back. Apart from that having a lovely time. Wish
you were here.*

I keep them all, you know, she'd said. I sometimes
sit and read them, one after the other. Or I shuffle
them and deal one. Like a tarot card message for
the day.)

Story of. Richard wonders what will happen
now to all those postcards from their imaginary
child.

Recycling bin.

He shrugs.

As he thinks it, an email appears in his inbox.

Subject: Re: our mother's memorial service

Dear Richard

very sorry but its close family only who will be
speaking at the memorial. Will pass on the
suggestion about the poem thank you but it is
already a v busy programme. It is shaping up to be
a v special day. Look fwd see you Friday, vbw
Dermot and Patrick Heal.

He sits back in his chair.

Don't go, the imaginary daughter says.

How can we not? he says.

We don't need to, she says.

I can't not. I have to honour her, he says.

So do something that'll really honour her, she says.

On a Saturday evening in October, a couple of days before he gets on a train north thinking naively that getting on a train to somewhere else means he'll be able to escape himself or survive himself, Richard finally opens the latest Terp email.

These are the new draft scenes.

He's supposed to have read and annotated them by yesterday for discussion at Monday's meeting.

There are ten. He opens the first. It's set in a cable car.

<u>EXT. CABLE CARS IN SNOWY</u>
<u>MOUNTAINS. AFTERNOON</u>

The cable cars have all come to a halt. The cable car containing Katherine and Rainer sways a little

on its cable. A crow caws in the
trees.

<u>INT. RAINER AND KATHERINE'S
CABLE CAR IN SNOWY MOUNTAINS.
CONTINUOUS. AFTERNOON</u>

Rainer regards Katherine from the
opposite wooden bench.

RAINER
I did not think to find such a love
in Switzerland. Who knew this
country would give me such a gift?
I have written a poem for you.
Tonight I will recite it to you.

Katherine smiles. She closes her
eyes. She opens them again.

RAINER
I would like to place a rose petal
on each of your eyelids. I would like
you to wake to their coolness, and
the roses to wake equally to your
eyes that send their warmth into
nature even when they are closed and
you are asleep. I am a lover of
roses too you know. I would like

roses to enter you and you to enter
roses. Now. Close your eyes.

Katherine considers him for a moment
with her eyes. Then she obediently
closes her eyes.

EXT. CABLE CARS IN SNOWY MOUNTAINS.
CONTINUOUS. AFTERNOON

INT. JOHN'S CABLE CAR.
CONTINUOUS. AFTERNOON

John, coming down from Montana,
notices Katherine and Rainer in the
static cable car across from his own.
At first he is pleased. They must be
coming up to see him. He knocks on
the glass of his cable car to try to
attract their attention.

JOHN
Tig! Tig darling!

EXT. JOHN'S CABLE CAR. CONTINUOUS.
AFTERNOON

John can be seen behind the glass
shouting hello, but not being heard.

The sound of wind, crows cawing.
He bangs his hand silently on the
glass.

A moment later John sees something
that he'd rather not see.

He bangs both his hands, and then
his whole body, against the glass of
the cable car.

EXT. CABLE CARS. CONTINUOUS.
AFTERNOON

One cable car in the sequence of
hanging cars is swaying about quite
violently.

INT. RAINER AND KATHERINE'S
CABLE CAR.
CONTINUOUS. AFTERNOON

Katherine and Rainer, who has his
hand inside Katherine's dress inside
her coat, surface from their kiss.
Katherine notices first, then Rainer,
the violently swaying cable car
across from theirs with the man in
it battering the glass in silence.

                    RAINER
    It doesn't look safe. It looks like
      it might - Good God. Katherine.
    I think that's your husb - isn't
             that your -?

     EXT. RAINER AND KATHERINE'S
              CABLE CAR.
        CONTINUOUS. AFTERNOON

Katherine presses herself hard
against the glass, with Rainer out of
focus behind her. Katherine's face is
terrified.

Oh for Christ sake.
He puts his hands over his eyes. He groans out
loud. He shuts his laptop lid.
He reaches the novel down from the pile of books
on the shelf above the TV. April, by Bella Powell.
He opens it somewhere in the middle.

for it was the gong sounding dinner time again,
again, hurry down! hurry down! calling the guests
to dress for dinner, dress for the pristine whiteness
of the tablecloths, hurry down to the Salle à Manger
of the Grand Hotel Château Bellevue with its floor
tiles so clean that the chair legs and table legs
reflected down into them suggesting there perhaps

existed another world on the underside of this world, another dining room, one balanced with an exact precision upside down beneath it, touching it at points of contact as yet mysterious, and these the entry points to another world, one full of our differently calibrated other possible selves, but a world unreachable from, yet still attached to, this quotidian one, and here was a moment's access to, a fleeting vision of, the entrance to that other world with all its possibilities. Because the Salle à Manger was a world where even quite clearly opposing worlds could run into one another, typically via something that could not be more run-of-the-mill, for instance, today, a dish of salmon at a grand hotel, just a dish of salmon at the far end of a hotel salle à manger; today the dresser at the end of the room was spread with such a dish, a huge salmon complete with head, surrounded on the dish by little crayfish coming off its sides like sun rays, and there underneath both the salmon and the crayfish were the petals of dozens of roses, on which the fishes were laid. It made *her* think of praise, and of gods, to see those little crayfish placed like that, for all the world as if adoring the great god salmon, it was by far the nicest thing that had happened to her today, a very nice supper, it turned even the July rain into a celebration. It made *him* think, when he thought of the mouth of that salmon in its served-up dead-eyed face, that even language is a kind of muteness, that everything is at an irrevocable distance; it made him wish to cross incomprehensible farnesses and yet simultaneously know he couldn't, he was hobbled, shackled. It was the nature of things, we are all shackled, hobbled. So they sat in the dining room at their separate tables, this writer and that, not knowing anything of what they had in common, balanced on the surface of the world as if on a surface of sheet ice they didn't know was there, frozen in high summer, and together quite separately they ate piece after piece of the pink flesh of the same single silver-scaled salmon. Look! she noticed, a red rose petal had travelled with the serving of fish on to the plate of the man sitting solo at the table next to hers, perhaps by mistake, or perhaps the round-faced piglet-pink Swiss serving-maid liked him especially, chose him, had given him this piece of pure colour on his plate especially, of course she herself had no petal, well, she tossed her head a little (though in truth she felt a touch sad she didn't have one of those bright red gifts of fortune on her own plate too) and she looked away as the man probed the petal with the tines of his fork – for they were utterly remote from each other, there were oceans between them in that same room sitting next to one another at their separate tables, tables made originally (though the people randomly sitting at them had no way of knowing this, nobody had, because it was not thought relevant to anything so never recorded by anyone anywhere) from the wood of the same one individual tree.

Richard lets the book shut in his hand, lets it fall on to the table.

I don't really need the money, he thinks. I can let this one go. I'll phone them on Monday and tell them. I'll phone tomorrow and leave a message on the office answerphone and they'll get it first thing Monday.

But this is the first thing he's been offered in nearly four years.

Hobbled, he thinks. Shackled.

He opens his laptop.

But he can't bear to open Terp's attachment again.

Instead, as if it's the same thing as working, he types into the search engine the words Rainer Maria Rilke followed by the words hobbled and shackled. Up comes a quite easy-to-read poem by R. M. Rilke. It's about a white horse galloping across a field in Russia in springtime, a horse full of *perfect joy* even though one of its legs has a hobble attached to it.

The poem's last line is about how images are gifts.

Oh, that's good.

He immediately wants to tell Paddy.

He looks over at Paddy's books, on the shelf above the TV too. He hasn't even looked at them since he brought them home that snowy day. He reaches them all down. He opens one at random.

In it, the real Katherine Mansfield is in Paris in the month of March, 1922. She is spending days going between a hotel and a clinic. Every day when she gets into the hotel lift the little boy who works the lift in this grand hotel tells her in French about the weather, regardless of whether she's about to go out into it or she's coming back in from it. If it's a rainy day, he tells her it's still winter. On the days when there's been sunlight, the little lift boy tells her it'll be full summer just a month from now.

The too-thin lady. The little lift boy.

Richard stays up into the early hours of Sunday reading here and there in these books, in which Katherine Mansfield, the real person, is writing letters to other real people.

In one of the books her brother has died in the war. In another her TB has just been diagnosed, bad in one lung, like being shot in one wing, she says (and when he reads this Richard can feel his own lungs inside him like two wings). The TB fills her with *the furies*. She goes to Switzerland for her health. *I have two rooms and a huge balcony, and so many mountains that I haven't even begun to climb them yet. They are superb.* She is, what's the word – sanguine. *One begins the wandering of a consumptive – fatal! Everybody does it and dies.*

She is dry and truthful. *I'm sick of people dying who promise well. One doesn't want to join that crowd at all.* At one point she writes at length to a doctor who's been treating her, to thank him for helping her know how to breathe, how to sit most comfortably, and how to keep her feet warm. She describes to him – *I wonder whether you might be interested* – a few details, things a tubercular patient has noticed about being tubercular. The patient treating the doctor, Richard thinks; how clever she is to know to switch roles, grant herself that bit of authority. Look how she describes herself stretching her arms when she wakes up, *imitating the actions of an opera singer who makes just this gesture before taking a high note which he wants to 'hold' as long as possible.* This, she tells the doctor, helps in times of fatigue; a thing that also helps, should a tubercular patient chance to feel depressed, is to *change your position.* A gentle humming under the breath *seems to break the feeling of 'isolation'.* Then she advises a conscious relaxation when it comes to facing a plate of food so as not to be terrified out of eating it by your own digestive system, and she ends her letter to the doctor by saying that when breathing *is very troublesome and the weather is dark I find it a help to look at pictures.*

The letter has a separate footnote beneath the end of it where the editors of the book of letters quote a funny limerick she's written earlier about this doctor: *A doctor who came from Jamaica/ Said: This time I'll mend her or break her./I'll plug her with serum/And if she can't bear 'em/I'll call in the next undertaker.*

He riffles the pages, lets them fall open. She hears there's a Russian doctor in Paris who can cure people with consumption outright by X-raying their spleens. He says he has cured 15,000 people. She tries to work out how to afford this doctor, who is very prestigious indeed, and clearly very rich. He sends her a letter telling her how much his seances, or sessions, cost. In it he uses the word guerison.

She writes to a friend on Christmas Day 1921 saying how much this word *shines.*

Richard doesn't know what guerison means.

He looks it up on Google Translate.

Healing, cure.

Of course, there's no cure for TB in being X-rayed. It's a joke. It's a swizz. The more he reads, the more he is angered on her behalf. He likes her, this woman who died a century ago. He likes her immensely. She is funny. *It has all been mush of a mushness.* She is brilliant, tricksy, arch, flirty, charming, and full of an unfathomable energy for someone so ill, full of black moods, yet *I always write as though I am laughing.* She finds Switzerland very laughable, but she likes it too, because *the 3rd class passenger is just as good as the 1st class passenger in Switzerland, and the shabbier you are the <u>less</u> you are looked at.* She is courageous beyond belief. She is fierce. *I feel as fastidious as though I wrote with acid.* She is generous. She sends an infatuated young writer, someone writing a fan letter to her and asking for advice, the name of a publisher; she says she'll write to the publisher for this young writer and tell him about him. She tells this young man, *I'm in love with life – terribly.* She apologizes for the unfashionableness of being so in love with life. Then she writes, *I am sending you a postcard of myself & the two knobs of the electric light. The photographer insisted they should be there as well.*

That night, when Richard eventually gets himself off to bed, he dreams he is a young writer and that he answers the door to his flat and a postman hands him a sheaf of letters and one of them is from a woman who has sent him a picture of herself with her hand on a light switch shaped like a breast, like she is demonstrating electricity by holding electricity's nipple.

It is unbelievably lovely.

He wakes up coming into his own hands.

He gets up, washes, drinks a glass of water, goes back to bed and back to sleep.

He sleeps well.

He wakes so late next day it's already afternoon.

He spends what's left of Sunday's daylight hours browsing online to see if he can find the image that will have been on that postcard Katherine Mansfield sent to the young writer, the one with the electric light switch somewhere in it. He looks in Google Images. He looks on eBay. He looks on some of the countless sites that come up when you look up her name and the word *postcard*. By the end of the afternoon he hasn't found the picture but he knows quite a lot about what some of the postcards Katherine Mansfield sent said.

It strikes him, as the dark comes down outside, that in paying this attention to Katherine Mansfield he has been neglecting the other writer, Rainer Maria Rilke.

So he types in, instead, just to see what will happen, *R. M. Rilke* followed by the word *postcard*.

Something does happen.

A series of sites comes up and each one tells a version of the same story, that a big reason R. M. Rilke even wrote one of his great works at all, a set of sonnets dedicated to Orpheus, in that turret in 1922, was that a lover of his had chanced to tack a postcard with a renaissance picture of the musician Orpheus on it to one of the walls in his writing room.

Orpheus, who went down into the underworld to

find his dead wife, and he did find her, and nearly rescued her, nearly brought her back to the surface, back to life, but then he ruined it by turning to look at her when he'd been told specifically not to, because looking back at what is behind you, if you're trying to get out of the world of the dead alive, is against the rules.

A couple of the internet sites reproduce the renaissance picture the poet had on his wall in postcard form. It's not that beautiful. It's not even that interesting. A curly-haired man wearing Roman-looking clothes and playing a stringed instrument is sitting in a tree that seems to have formed itself round him into an armchair. A small gathering of deer and rabbits is listening to him play.

It's not an image that would've moved Richard to write a work of art.

It's completely dark out now, the last October Sunday of summertime. Next week will be even darker. Richard puts the lights on all round his flat. As he moves from light switch to light switch he can feel the edges of himself all alive.

His lungs have started to hurt again too.

In the early evening he composes the following message. It takes him two hours to get right.

Dear Martin,

Thanks for the drafts.

To come straight to the point. If I'm to direct this

project I want us to go about this story quite another way.

With respect I must confess to having been uneasy all along at the form of fictionalizing of real people's lives that the script has taken thus far.

I'd like to suggest a radical departure.

Please hear me out.

I'm going to insist that if you want to work with me we approach this project differently and start over with a new script. Re this new script: I see it shaped formally as like a series of postcards from these writers' lives. By which I mean depiction of very slight moments from their lives that will act as revelations of depth.

This I think is more in keeping with the spirit of the book we are adapting and also with the truth of a relationship between two real people who did not know each other and about which and whom, even though they may be famous writers with seemingly well-documented lives, we still know next to nothing.

Also with the time we are portraying, the postcard being the most contemporary and popular way of being in touch at this point in time, rather like the text or email or even instantgram of today.

Also it gives us a way to use both image and text. As well as a way to gesture towards some of the other things happening at the time in history

*I mean in the world as it was – as well as to the
world as it is right now – but all of this with some
courtesy towards truth and to what we know and
don't know in this instance.*

*For instance you will know K. Mansfield's
little brother Leslie whom she loved beyond
belief died in 1915 in Belgium, when a grenade
he was teaching recruits how to throw blew up in
his hand.*

*And yet in 1918 she sends a postcard from
Cornwall to her friend Ida in London (who she
also sometimes as a pet name called Lesley, a
version of her brother's name) asking her to buy
her the brand of cigarettes specifically called
GRENADE. This is when she is already really
ill with tuberculosis just diagnosed, and these are
a particularly heavy duty kind of cigarette, it says
in the Col. Letters of K Mansfield. She was not an
unthinking user of words as I know from my own
lengthy perusal of her letters etc. This is just one
example. I am convinced there is mileage in this.
Images/moments – take this one – will radiate
by themselves with revelation of her spirit, anger,
desperation, defiance. As well as, here for instance,
the terrible unspoken story of the loss of the
brother.*

*Add to this what a picture postcard, depicting a
myth – Orpheus the mythical musician – meant to
R. M. Rilke. I am sure you will know already from*

your research that the great poems he wrote in 1922
were partly inspired or enabled by an image on a
postcard that his lover pinned on the wall in his
writing room. A postcard meant that all those great
poems somehow got themselves written.

The slightness of it gestures against the odds. It is
like a magic spell.

And this in itself is very like the fact of those two
writers just living in the same place at the same
time in their lives, whether they met or not.

This is the kind of coincidence that sends
electricity through the truths of our lives.

Our lives which often have what we might call a
postcard nature.

I hope you see what I am getting at?

I have always believed in not compromising the
form the drama takes by underestimating what its
natural potential offers.

I believe that if we pay this project the right and
true attention the outcome could be really
something. I feel that if we don't it will be a waste
and a lost chance.

Our April really could be something great.

Knowing this is a difficult letter to stomach. And
with respect.

Look forward to hearing from you,
all the best,
R.

Richard reads it over.

He removes the word lengthy from the word perusal; he decides he doesn't want to lie.

He makes the decision not to copy it to the office or the sponsors. He addresses it singly to Terp.

He reads it through once more and then, feeling a bit cavalier, he clicks the send box.

Remember Paddy and him at that big multimedia conference, Adjust Your Sets: The Future Is Spectacular, when was it, 1993? Onstage in one of the afternoon sessions a very young man, a graduate from Cambridge, was making a splash displaying a website (before very many people were even familiar with the word website) where he'd created and displayed the obituaries of people who'd never existed.

The young man was fashionable beyond self-doubt. He flashed up images on the big screen of gravestones, urns, photos of real people his website claimed were these 'dead' people, and of their families, their pets, their possessions. He displayed alongside this some of the messages that had come in from members of the public in response to the obituaries on the site.

They'd been truly moving, he said, deeply personal and responsive, real cries from the heart. A picture of a bicycle or a guitar that had 'belonged' to a 'dead' person could move strangers all over the world to tears.

But why? Richard had asked when it came to audience questions. Why are you doing this? Why go out of your way to create any of this at all?

To demonstrate what people will write or send when they contact the website, the young man said. People *like* feeling. They like to be asked to feel. Feeling is a very powerful thing. I've already been approached by numerous advertisers keen to advertise on Mourning Has Broken.

Do the people who respond to your, your, website, do they *know* that these people you're displaying as having so sadly passed away are all completely made up? Richard said.

We explain that the profiles are fictional prototypes in the small print of the terms and conditions for initial log-in on the website, the man said. You have to log in if you want to send us a message. Which also means we have, as by-product, an expanding list, it's called a database, of personal information about our website members.

But you're lying, someone else in the audience said. You're lying about life, about the deaths, and about emotional connection.

No, I'm storytelling, the young man said. The emotional connection is true. And it's very very valuable.

But you're pretending it's real, and it isn't, the woman holding the microphone said.

It is real, the young man said. It's real if you think it is.

Paddy, sitting next to Richard, stood up. She waited for the microphone to be passed to her.

What you've just said about reality and thought is, if we're talking philosophically, both interesting and bankrupt, she said. And very clever. It's the ultimate immorality.

It's a new morality, Terp onstage beneath the massive image of the graveyard had said.

Congratulations, Paddy said. You're going to make a lot of money.

And not just for me, Terp said.

It makes me want to cry just seeing it, the next person who had the microphone said. Even though I know you've just made up that person and they've never died or anything. It makes me feel for what will be my own death, and for all the people I know who are going to die. Thank you.

No, thank *you*, Terp had said. Thank you for your feedback.

Far in the past, Richard, incredulous, is shaking his head.

Far in the future, Richard has just ordered a steak on Deliveroo on his Mastercard.

It's touch and go as to whether any of his cards will work these days. But the order goes through. After he's eaten, he'll look up online some of

Katherine Mansfield's fiction. He really ought to read some now.

He spends his suppertime online trying to unsubscribe from a site he's visited once and which now sends his inbox three advertising emails a day, a site on which every time you click the unsubscribe link you're sent to a blank page. He is cramming the food delivery packaging into the binbag by the front door when his inbox lights up across the room. He doesn't hurry back. It'll be Dibs.com sending him more messages about things he never wanted to buy in the first place to prove to someone or something somewhere how much advertising clout Dibs.com has.

It's a message from Terp.

He sits down. He opens it.

Subject : Insta-grandad

Thank you you Dick for your email. The <u>really exciting</u> news is we've found an actress who thinks she actually *is* Katharine Mansfield. I mean really her reincarnated – yeah she psychotically believes herself to be her. I'm not joking. And she is AMAZING. The vibe that comes off her is so strong. She says she even tried to contract TB herself once so she could more authentically feel the whole experience! Mad eh mate! Pleased to say I am alrcady getting spectacularly good feedback on the new drafts, backers readers are <u>loving</u> them I've also been requested by broadcaster to include more varied ethnicity in the project and am looking at range of new hotel worker characters/visiting dignitary guests to tick those boxes any inspiration here v welcome. Thanks etc for all ideas etc all ideas always welcome looking forward to your feedback and to seeing you tomorrow PLUS I've just been reading up on 1940s in Swiss sanatoriums where people got sent into coma on and off for a year as sleep cure and how if they did this they might wake up not just cured but also looking 20 years younger for the record. !! something you'd like to try yourself Dick? ;) Think I can work it into script. What if she never died or not till the 1970s or something? – turnup for the books eh! Yes we can change history

    till tomorrow

    MT

    Terp has deleted Richard's original email from the bottom of this one and copied this reply to the broadcaster, the backers, and everybody at the office.

    Insta-grandad

    Thank you you Dick

    something you'd like to try yourself

    Cheeky little fucker.

    Richard breathes in.

    It hurts.

    He breathes out.

It hurts.

A horse hoof with a wooden peg nailed through it, seen up close.

A letter, unfolded, with a word in it in another language which shines so strongly that the light that comes off it lights a dark room.

A small boy manning a lift in a grand hotel. Here comes the dying woman again. What can he give her today? His forehead creases; you can see the lines form in it.

With his own head full of the wasted images Richard shuts the lid of his laptop.

11.59.

The station automaton announces the arrival of a train. It tells him that ScotRail apologizes for the late running of the service and for any inconvenience caused.

Richard is sorry too. He'd like to apologize. He knows he is being as clichéd as a character in a Terp drama. But what can he say? He is sorry, sorry, sorry. He is sorry.

He also knows he is and will be being recorded by CCTV cameras on both sides of the station. He knows these are the kinds of cameras that don't know anything, don't show anything beyond surface. He knows that what they do is the stupid new way of knowing everything.

He is pretty sure he can move faster than any people who may or may not be paying attention to

CCTV images wherever those people may be in the station. It's as if those images the cameras will take of him, though they haven't even happened yet, are already somewhere behind him. They belong to posterity. They're not about now.

He also knows, and he's sorry, that he will be leaving a mess for someone else to clear up after him.

He doesn't know what else to do.

Sorry.

He is ten years old, a boy with his arms out wide from his sides, not playing aeroplanes like the other post-war boys, no, his arms are not wings, or about flight. What they've become is the long flexible pole of a boy on a tightrope as high as the clouds (so high the clouds sometimes dampen his fringe).

He is balancing against air on a wire as thin as the stuff inside his father's fishing reels. His father is a man who, though that war is more than a decade in the past, more than a lifetime ago to his son, wakes up shouting in the middle of the night, then gets up and batters himself against the doors of the big wardrobe his parents have in their room.

He himself, on the other hand, has achieved a near-impossible standard for a boy of ten, of balance and height against the odds.

Now Richard is in his thirties, in bed with the woman who'll become his wife. When is this? More than thirty years ago. His future wife, in his arms,

is crying because spring, her favourite season,
is over.

You can't cry about summer coming, he says.
I could understand you crying about winter. But
summer?

I can cry about anything I like, she says.

He is surprised. Can people just do that, cry
about anything they like? He wishes it held true for
him. He can never cry about anything.

His future wife, rubbing her face against his chest
hair to dry her eyes, which feels actually very erotic,
and sex quite often does make her cry in their early
days together, tells him that after she's dead she's
going to come back every year as blossom on a tree.

And if you die before me, he says, I will spend all
the time I'm alive and not with you negotiating the
various time differences across the world so that I
can spend as much time as a man possibly can on
this planet in springtime, in search of you.

She bursts into tears again when he says it. He
feels very romantic.

Five years on from this spring promise he'll walk
through their house towards the shattered panel of
glass in the back door some days after something's
been thrown at it (the kettle? the cat?), because the
whole door is now a frosted jigsaw of fragments,
and since it's one of the light sources for much of
downstairs, and he'll sell the house all the years
later without ever having had it repaired, it'll be like

the house is stuck in winter light for nearly a decade no matter the actual season.

Now? He is a man at a station waiting for his last train.

The seasons are meaningless.

No – worse than meaningless. Paddy is rubble, and time just keeps on going. Autumn, then there'll be winter. Then there'll be spring, and so on.

He looks down at the rails, the neat-keptness of their pattern. He looks at the ground round about them, the stony stuff and grass round the neatness.

I'm rubble too, he thinks. Just in a different form. The whole world and all its people. Rubble.

So shouldn't we be treating the world better? the imaginary daughter says in his head. Since it's so much *us*? Since we're so literally made of *it*?

My darling, you're imaginary, he says.

Yeah, I know, she says.

You don't exist, he says.

And yet here I am, she says.

Go away, he says.

How can I? she says. I'm you.

That's when the train appears down the track. It approaches. It draws level. It stops. Its doors beep.

Only the very back set of doors opens; nobody else is getting off except these two people he passes, a girl and a woman, one white, one mixed race, the woman in some kind of uniform, thick trenchcoat, the girl in schoolclothes that look too thin for the north of Scotland. The story about them, whatever it is, starts to spark away but on the worst terms, nothing but outer appearance.

Extinguish it.

What a relief, to be finished, finished with it all for good, and he passes them by, they've become nothing but rubble too, same as everything else, right now they're really useful ballast because they're blocking the view between him and a station guard, a woman in high-vis who's come out to meet the train.

There's not much room to fit a body under. This train is pretty close to the ground. Its metal, down here at the less visible level, is caked with mud. Even the machine has to encounter nature, not even it can escape the earth. There's something reassuring in that.

He bends to the train's, what's the word? Underneath. Underside.

If he gets his body down prone on the ground he can get his head – he looks to see where the wheels are. He lies down on his front. Stones. Grass. Metal. He turns over. He tries to get his head near the wheel with the back of his neck against the rail.

In less than a minute from now several people in high-vis will be running towards the end of the platform from the station offices.

But right now, nothing. A moment of nothing. Another moment of nothing.

You'd think a late train would leave a station faster.

The underside of a train drips with a kind of truth. Well, to be more truthful, with filthy water. He closes his eyes.

Any second now he will stop time in its tracks.

Any second now time'll be over.

Any second now.

—

Hey.

Hey. Sir.

He opens an eye. One of the drips hits him in it. He lifts a hand to rub it and bangs the back of it on something metal, jerks his head when he does and hits his forehead hard off the underside of the train.

Ow.

Excuse me, sir.

He wrenches his head out from under the train.

A girl, a real one, the one who'd just got off this train, is crouched on the edge of the platform along from the back of the train. She is looking straight at him.

I really need you not to do that, she says.

February. The first bee hits the window glass.

The light starts to push back, stark in the cold. But birdsong rounds the day, the first and last thing as the light comes and goes.

Even in the dark the air tastes different. In the light from the streetlight the branches of the bare trees are lit with rain. Something has changed. No matter how cold it is that rain's not winter rain any more.

The days lengthen.

That's where the word Lent comes from.

In Latin the name of the month derives from words about how to purify, how to appease the gods, usually by burnt offerings, probably both etymologically sourced in Februa, the Roman feast of purification. Vegetation month, month of the return of the sun, rain-month, cabbage-sprouting month, month of ravenous wolves, month of cakes offered to the gods for a good year, good harvest, good life.

In the Highlands of Scotland, back when traditions were more closely followed than they are now, it was the month when people lit candles to call the sun back to the earth (the source of Candlemas); at this time of the year girls would model shapes out of the last sheaves of the last harvest's corn, place their creations in a cradle and dance round the cradle singing a song about life coming back, about the snakes waking and leaving their nests, the birds returning, about St Bride, or Brigid, or Bridget of Kildare, patron saint of, among many things, Ireland, fertility, the season of spring, pregnant women, blacksmiths and poets, cows and milkmaids, mariners and boatmen, midwives and illegitimate children. A version of a celtic fire goddess called Brid, in whose honour people used to light bonfires, she was also a blesser of holy wells and places whose water is still said to have the power to cure ailments, especially of the eyes.

Whatever her name was, she took her father's sword which was studded with jewels and gave it away to the local lepers. They gouged out the jewels and sold them for food. She gave her father back his empty sword.

Then she asked an Irish king to give her some

land she could build an abbey on, where a community of women could live and dedicate themselves to charity.

But the king wasn't listening. He was looking at her breasts.

When he saw her see him looking, he looked instead at the little cape she was wearing over her shoulders.

Will you give me as much land as this cape I'm wearing will cover? she said.

The king laughed. Okay, he said.

She took the cape off and put it down on the ground. The cape began to spread. It grew and it grew. Brigid took one corner. Three other versions of Brigid took the other corners. They started walking, one east, one west, one north and one south.

Brigid herself went north. She crossed a field of mud. Wherever she stepped, wherever her feet touched the ground, flowers sprang up out of the nothing there.

2

Now don't go getting us wrong.

We want the best for you. We want to make the world more connected. We want you to feel the world is yours. We want you to see the world through us. We want you to be yourself. We want you to feel a little less alone. We want you to find others just like you.

We want you to know we're your best source of knowledge in the world. We want to know everything about you. We want to know about all the places you go. We want to know where you are right now. We want you to post images of what it is you're looking at so you will remember this special moment always. We want you to take a look at what you posted ten years ago right now. Happy Anniversary! We want to remind you regularly of the special moments you've had in the past. We want to show you what your friends were posting ten years ago right now. We want you to record your lives because your lives mean so much. We want you to know you mean something in the world. We want you to know how much you mean to us. We want you to know we're very interested in what matters to you. We want you to know it matters to us too.

We want to count every step you take. We want to help you be fit and strong. We want to know what makes your heart beat faster. We want you to send us a sample of your DNA and a sum of money so we can help you find out who you are, who your family is and was and where you came from in history, and we want it only for these totally legitimate reasons as a useful service to you.

We want you to be everything that you can be: friends, in a relationship, single, and complicated. We want to know what you buy. We want to know what music you're listening to on your headphones. We want to know what you're wearing. We want to tailor our advertising bespoke to you. We want it to be right for you. We want you to find out more about yourself. We want you to take our fun psychological personality test to find out what kind of person you really are and who you'll vote for in elections. We want to be able to categorize you precisely for helpful input for other people's fun projects as well as our own.

We want to be there in your living room. We want to help you sort out everyday little problems like where to eat, where to stay on holiday, where a film is showing and at what times, where lots of people near you are having a really good time right now. We want to help you with the chore of ordering things online: catfood, gardening things, things for your children. We want to help you with general knowledge for your children. We want you to think of us as a family member. We're interested in everything you say. We want to hear what you say every time you look at a screen. We want to be able to see you through that screen while you're looking at something entirely other than us. We want to know what you say to each other in every room in your house. We want to know what hours you keep, what you spend them doing when you're online and when you aren't, and how you spend your money.

We want the phones we sell to you to work more slowly and less well than the previous models, so that you'll want to buy a newer model sooner.

We want to hire people to attack anyone powerful who says stuff about us that we don't like, regardless of whether it's true. We want the black and Latino people who work for us to feel a little less important and protected and able to rise in the company hierarchy than the white people, though we want them to give us their helpful input when it comes to dealing with ethnicity data too.

We want to stand up for freedom of speech, especially for powerful rich white people. We want to help millions of people to read posts by trolls. We want to help with government propaganda and to help people skew elections, and not to hinder people organizing and promoting ethnic cleansing, all as helpful by-products of being there 24/7 for you.

We want you to know how much your face means to us. We want your face and the faces of everyone you photograph and the faces of all your friends and the faces of the people they photograph recorded online on our sites for our fun data archive and research.

We want you to know we're keeping you safe. We want you to know we respect and protect your privacy. We want you to know we believe privacy is a human right and a civil liberty, especially if you can afford it. We want to assure you that you have control. We want you to know what good control you have over who can see your information. We want you to know you have full access to your information – you and anyone who shadows you.

We want to narrate your life. We want to be the book of you. We want to be the only connection that matters. We want it to be inconvenient for you not to use us. We want you to look at us and as soon as you stop looking at us to feel the need to look at us again. We want you not to associate us with lynch mobs, witchhunts or purges unless they're *your* lynch mobs, witchhunts and purges.

We want your pasts and your presents because we want your futures too.

We want all of you.

Any time at all. Here, take it. Take my face.

I'm not surprised you want my face. It's the face of now.

What I mean by my face is the face on this A4 photocopy, the proof I exist. Without it I officially don't. Even though I'm bodily here, without this piece of paper I'm not. If I lose it, wherever I am I won't be anywhere. It's getting a bit worn – not surprising, just an A4-size sheet of paper – and because it's folded at the place where the face happens to be copied on it, some of the photocopier ink that makes my face has flaked off in the crease of the fold.

But I'm here. I exist because this piece of paper with my face on it proves I'm not able to study here or work here or live here without permission or earn any money here.

125

My being ineligible makes you all the more eligible.

No worries. Happy to help.

Also you'll notice this face resembles the drawings on the posters that tell you to report anything you think looks suspicious.

Tell the police if you see anyone who looks like me, because my face is of urgent matter to your nation.

Not at all. No problem. Glad to be of service.

And it's this face, like the faces on the poster-lorry the white man in the suit posed in front of, of a great queue of people, I mean non-people, at a border, which proved once and for all that all the people on the poster were faceless nobodies while his was the face of a somebody. He had the only face that matters.

My face is a breaking point.

Don't mention it. Any time.

It's the face you see on dramas, films, or you picture in your head in the novels about people who aren't you, the books you read because you love literature, or to kill some free time, the ones that tell the stories that let you feel that you've felt, you've been really importantly moved, more, you've understood something major about the history, the politics, of the time you live in.

It's nothing. My pleasure. My face is all about you.

My face trodden in mud.
My face bloated by sea.
What my face means is not your face.
By all means. You're welcome.

**It was September Brittany Hall first heard of the
girl,** the morning when Stel from Welfare went past
her in staff lockers and told her, listen, Brit, age of
miracles isn't past, some schoolkid got into the
centre and – you won't believe it. I still can't. She
got management to clean up the toilets.

Management to what? Brit said.

Then she said: how do you mean, *she*?

Kids weren't as such that unusual. The CIOs
often sent people here they'd designated adult who
were plainly still kids, thirteen, fourteen. But this
was a male-only centre.

All of the toilets, Stel said. Every single pan in
every room on every wing, even isolation. I don't
mean management personally, management
cleaning the shitters, shite for sore eyes. I mean it,
a kid. A girl. Twelve or thirteen, I didn't see her

129

myself. I haven't spoken to anyone who did with their own eyes. But she got in. Not just that. Got all the way to management. Got them to bring in a cleaning company to do it, I mean *really* do it, between the tiles, the cracks and the staining, all the stuff the cleaner-detainees can't get clean any more, and they came in with these great big pressure cleaners, steam cleaners like at the car handjob places and they did all the pans and all the tiles and surrounds and then they mopped it all up afterwards, God, smells so much better in there, wait till you get on the wing, they did all the wings, whole H block. Some of the detainees've seen her too, school uniform, wandering about by herself on B wing, everybody standing back looking like what the fuck.

You are shitting me, Brit said.

Shit's all gone, Stel said. Ta daa. Like magic. Even off the walls in constant watch.

No shit, Brit said.

That's it, Brit. Innit? No shit, Stel said.

You're a poet, Brit said, and you don't know it.

I do know it, Stel said. I just don't get much chance these days to use it. But today? Today, oh, me, I'm full of it today. Poetry I mean.

She went off down the corridor singing lines from oh what a beautiful morning using the corridor echo so the song went from one end to the other. She waved to Brit with one hand while she waved to the camera so they'd let her through security with the other.

Stel'd been working here years, three years someone said, as long as that. She was nearly thirty. Brit herself was relatively new. Deets could still tell. This wasn't a good thing. *I congratulate you that you are here four months same as me, and you are not dead, and I am not dead, we are both not dead yet DCO Miss Hall*, one of the Syrians, every day, teasing her. It was kindly meant. But kindly meant was complicated. There were lines you had to draw. There were correct responses. On the one hand there was laugh and say something funny back, on the other there was how dare you talk to me like that. It depended.

Body cams. Razor wire. Deets.

(Stel for instance never said deets. Stel being black herself got checked more than the not-black staff every time she left the centre to go home. Even though everybody knew Stel. Stel was patience itself. You'd have to be. Doing what she did every day.)

Imagine a child on the wing.

Actually Brit quite often imagined a child on the wing, because of how they describe the weight restriction of personal possessions per deet across detention estate. 25kg, same as the weight of a small child three or four years old, so whenever the new deets arrived she'd use it as a reminder to herself, does that look more or less than the weight of a small child? because if it looks a lot more they'll be kicking off any minute when it's taken from them.

Not detention estate as in housing estate. More like when Brit's father died and they talked about his estate and it meant what's left of you in terms of what you're worth after you die.

This made the place that pays her a salary like a kind of underworld, she thought. Place of the living dead. The gate to her underworld was the new little rows of hedge sprigs in the boxes they'd put at the front between the car park and the building to smarten or maybe soften the place up for visitors arriving. Every day now, going into work then leaving for home at the end of the shift, she nodded at them, DMZ between underworld and rest of world.

Hello, hedges. (Wish me luck.)

Goodbye, hedges. (Another day done.)

She went inside on the knowledge. She left on the knowledge. The knowledge was, she could leave. She could leave at the end of every day (or morning, if she was on nights).

But she was sort of always there even when she wasn't. Even though she could leave, and at the end of the shift she just did, went out, past those hedges, cross the road, cross the car park, walk along the airport road to the station and get on the train, get home.

What do they make you do there? her mother said when she'd been a fortnight into the job.

I'm a DCO at one of the IRCs employed by the private security firm SA4A who on behalf of the HO run the Spring, the Field, the Worth, the Valley, the Oak, the Berry, the Garland, the Grove, the Meander, the Wood and one or two others too, she said.

Brittany, her mother said. What language are you speaking?

Brit wasn't stupid. She'd been good at languages. She'd been good at everything at school without trying. She'd wanted college, but they couldn't afford it now. Be sensible. They couldn't have ever. But her mother gave herself a hard time over that not happening. So Brit never complained. Whenever she got home, *how was work?* Fine. *What did you do today?* Stuff, you know, the usual. Then you give a little laugh.

As long as you had a laugh, her mother said. Hard work and laughter go together like seaside and bad weather.

I'm finding that out all right, Brit said.

Then her mother said one day,

Brittany, what's a deet?

Had she really said deet out loud to her mother? Deet was a Torquil word, what he called them. But not unpleasantly. Torq was all right.

Deet, Brit said to him, in her first week.

I mean the actual stuff. It's an insect repellent, you know.

Uh huh, he said.

But the joke's on us, then, she said. If they're the deets.

Uh huh, Torquil said.

You calling them deets makes us the insects, she said.

Uh huh, Torquil said.

The bloodsuckers, she said.

Uh huh, Torquil said.

She laughed.

Uh huh, Torquil said.

Torq was Scottish which was why he had the funny name.

I'll explain, he said. Everything about this job is repellent. And you got to be careful with Deet. Your speech can get slurred, you can feel really sick, it's a neurotoxin, under your skin going right into you. Numbness, coma. Just warning you early on so you can monitor yourself for the signs, Britannia.

Brittany, what's a deet?

Oh, you know. (Laugh) Slang. Short for the word detail.

How was work, then?

Fine.

What did you do today?

The usual. Stuff. (Little laugh)

As long as you had a laugh. Hard work and laughter.

Her mother turned back to the 24-hour news channel. She shook her head like she does every day at the stuff happening.

So many destabilizing things happening in the world, she said.

It's just the news, mum, Brit said. It's rubbish.

Her mother always thought the news mattered. Everyone knew nowadays it wasn't what you watched to find out what was really happening. Except her mother. She still believed in TV. Old people did.

Wonder what on earth'll happen, her mother said.

Her mother hadn't a clue about the real world. Hard work, laughter. Not that there wasn't a lot of laughing at work. There was the laughing from deets that sounded like something had broken, and the laughing at deets from certain DCOs, laughter closer to the bone, threat-laughter. There was a lot of noise generally: laughing, crying, banging doors, thumping doors, shouting. It was a noisy job. Unless you were on scanning or recep or visits room. Make 'em laugh, make 'em cry, make 'em wait: whenever a deet laughed in that mad way that's what Torq said, make 'em wait all right: there wcrc people in here, in a place designed when it was first built for 72-hour detention at the most, who'd been here for years, years and years.

Seventy two hours? Three days.

Most of them in here'd been in at least a couple of months.

Hello, hedges.

Goodbye, hedges.

Day after day.

But *that* day? The whole place was different.

It was weird-quiet.

Nobody laughed. Nobody cried. Nobody, deets or DCOs, banged the doors.

The story went round.

A kid, a girl wearing a school uniform, apparently just *walked into* the centre.

First, it's not possible to do that. Nobody can, at this centre, or any centre. Just walk in. Not possible full stop. Here – and this isn't the tightest security place – you've got to be searched, checked, photographed, checked, assigned the visitor lanyard, checked, scanned, checked again, then security gates, doors, fences, doors, three more checks then wing recep final check.

Word went round that this kid had also walked in – and out – at four other IRCs.

Lies, Brit said. Fake news.

Then she saw the toilet in the room the Turk and the Pole deets Adnan and Tomek were in.

Then some other toilets in B wing.

They were really clean.

Is this, like, a giant April fool's thing? she said to

Dave. In fucking September? Is it some kind of SA4A test?

Dave hadn't seen the girl with his own eyes but he'd heard some of the stories doing the rounds. He told them to Brit at coffee. Then she was on visits room that afternoon and heard some more of the stories from Russell, who thought like she did that they were a bunch of total wank.

The story went that the girl had also, get this, rung a doorbell on one of the knocking houses in Woolwich, had got in there, and had come out again alive and unhad.

What, even in a school uniform? Brit said.

She and Russell laughed like drains.

The story went that the bent police had been called in by the pimps. *Come and get her. Take her,* they said. *Please. She's fucking ruining us.* Because she'd got in there and in the space of half an hour had gone through several rooms persuading clients out of doing what they were in the middle of doing, well that was pretty funny in itself, and then she'd made the guy on the front door unlock it and fifteen teenage and younger girls got free and ran for it, ran for their lives.

Yeah.

Right.

The story also went that one of the self-harmer deets, an Eritrean on C wing, Brit didn't know him, had looked up and found the girl in his room just standing there like a vision *like the fucking Virgin Mary* (Russell). The Eritrean self-harmer had said to her, this place they are keeping me in is like living in hopelessness, so why would I live? Only pain is keeping me alive. Then the schoolgirl'd said something back to him, though he wouldn't tell anyone what, and now he was like a new man. Russell and Brit spent ten minutes making up things she'd said to him, all of it obscene. Garbage, Brit said. How did she even get as far as C wing with nobody throwing her out? She's got wings, Russell said. Flew like an angel, little teenage sanitary towel wings on her heels.

The story also went that the girl's mother was a deet in the Wood, that her mother'd been picked up by the HO because she'd applied to do a course at a uni, she'd grown up here but she'd no passport and the HO picked her up off the street, she'd nipped out for ten minutes, gone down to the Asda, no coat on, bag of shopping left on the pavement when they picked her up. And then this girl had got herself into the Wood after the mother'd been in a few weeks and the girl had stood there telling the guys on the gate to sort it that night, get the DCOs to unlock her mother's room and then unlock the unit and then shut off the system and let her mother out.

Course they did, Brit said. We'd all do it. They just have to ask nicely.

She and Russell laughed like drains.

But.

Listen.

Apparently.

There'd been an internal breach at the Wood and some people got out and there *was* no visual. But CCTV playback from opposite the front gates shows some woman in the middle of the night just walking out of the Wood and a couple of others with her too.

Brit laughed. It was better than comedy. She laughed and laughed. She laughed so much and so loud that the people visiting the deets up and down the room turned and stared. She had to stop herself laughing.

Then she walked back up the room to make sure no deets were touching or sitting next to anybody. Sitting next to family is forbidden.

But the story bollocks got bigger and bigger all day.

It spread through the whole H block.

Someone, one of the secretaries, had overheard through a door what the girl had said to management.

She was in there for ten minutes at the most, Sandra (Oates's secretary) told Brit and a couple of others (plus Torq, honorary female) in the Staff Ladies.

Sandra spoke in a whisper, though all the toilet stall doors were open and no one else was in there.

She said it all calm and reasonable, Sandra said. She went so quiet I couldn't hear much, though I could hear the word why, the occasional why I could hear. It wasn't like I was eavesdropping, I was listening out in case I had to call security. But she'd already walked right past *them* no trouble, they hadn't stopped her, she walked past them as easy as she walked right past me, she gave me a straight look, I can't call it anything other than that, I didn't stop her, I didn't want to, and she knocked on his door and went right in and sat and waited for him. Then he went in. I tried to stop him and warn him but he was in one of his fuck off Sandra moods.

Then, what, five, ten minutes later, she comes out of the office and says, *goodbye Sandra, thank you very much*, I don't know how she knew my name but she did. And when she was gone he called me into the office, he'd gone all red, and he sent me to my desk to call up Steamclean and get them in ASAP.

The story went, Sandra said under her breath in the Ladies, that this girl had been visiting several other IRCs and persuading people to do all sorts of unorthodox things like cleaning toilets properly.

What did she look like? Brit said.

Like a schoolgirl, Sandra said. Like you see on the bus.

Sandra took them into her office and showed them the CCTV playback on the computer.

Sandra's office is really nice, like a normal office. Sandra let them peek inside Oates's office as well, really nicely furnished and very roomy.

On the playback they saw the top of the head of a quite small girl walking around.

She just walked around, like she was meant to be there. Nobody stopped her. When a door in front of her was shut she waited till it opened for some other reason and just walked through it. It was so plain and simple when they watched it that it just wasn't a mystery. A door opens. She goes through it.

Then Brit's shift was over.

She could leave.

She went for the train.

She sat and stared out its window. Her eyes went from what was outside the window to the marks and smudges on the surface of the window, the ones on the inside, the ones on the outside, back to the world beyond the marks on the window.

Some staff at work had been saying they knew about the girl, that she went to a Co-op academy with a friend of someone else at work's kids.

Some of the deets had been saying they'd heard of the girl, knew who she was. She'd survived a dinghy and come up from Greece.

No, she'd crossed a desert past skeletons who hadn't made it, kept herself alive by drinking her own urine.

She'd crossed the world wearing her little brother's Man United football shirt.

They said they knew her father, and that her father was dead, an important man in politics at the wrong time in the wrong place.

They said they knew her mother, that she'd been drowned in a boat off Italy.

They said she'd been bombed out, family had had to run for their life, guerrillas had used them as donkeys, made them all carry the encampment for miles, for days, and when her father had stopped and asked for a rest on the first day the guerrillas had said, here is your rest, and had shot him there and then.

Which is when Brit, who'd been listening to one of the men telling this story, had found herself glancing over, couldn't help it, at the South Sudan deet, Pascal, eyes down, head low on his neck, saying nothing. His casenotes said he claimed he'd been made not just to watch his father and brother both decapitated but been forced to choose which head he'd play football with, and to do it too.

But what astonished Brit on her way home on the train was what came into her own head when she thought about the girl.

It was a vision of her own mother.

In this vision, Brit's mother, bewildered, was in lockdown in a unit in the Wood. She was sitting on the plastic bedding looking at the drainhole in the floor. The smell coming through that drainhole was actually visible to Brit when she saw her mother's face in that vision.

The Wood, everyone knows, is rough on the women there, like living in a shower room with a bunch of strangers. Worse, the body searches. The assaults that never make it to report. The story goes, rapes. Course there are. Brit had heard it, they'd all heard it. No smoke. Plus, the women who'd been sex-trafficked across the world and ended up at the Wood all swore it. Detention there was worse than any of the rest of what had happened to them.

Brit shook her head to clear it.

Her mother was fine.

Her mother was at home watching the parliamentary channel on TV saying out loud to herself in an empty room, *wonder what'll happen.*

Leave it behind.

That's when she realized she'd forgotten today to say the goodbye to the stupid hedges.

Damn.

She was superstitious about it. Stupid really.

She thought about the little dark green leaves. Hedge smell. The smell of good bitterness. She thought how it wouldn't take long, no time at all, for those fairly new separate little hedge sprigs next to each other in their boxes, they were more than sprigs now, bushes already, to form into just the one hedge instead of all the separate plants they'd been planted as.

Say it now in your head like you'd say it to them.

Goodbye, hedges.

Another day done.

Yeah, but.

Quite a day.

Girl on the wing.

Total myth.

Utter bollocks.

But it was true, the toilets throughout, or on the wing she was on anyway, had definitely been deep-cleaned.

Good. Someone doing something right.

About fucking time.

One afternoon –

this is Torq telling her the story of the only other day that'd been anything like this one, way before her time, a day from back when he was a newbie himself –

I'd been here about six weeks. Four o clock. I was on break, we were in the staffroom, and there was this weird noise through the wing, it got louder, it was, like, a wave when you watch a wave bigger than the other waves coming in on the sea, then we realized it was the deets, it was the deets laughing. We looked at each other. It wasn't crazy laughing or drug laughing or fight laughing, it was a whole different kind of laughing. We were all, like, <u>what</u>?

So we got into riot gear.

The deets were crammed into every room with a working TV and they were all watching this old

*black and white film. I could see over their heads.
The silent movie guy with the Hitler moustache
and the bowler hat was sitting on a kerb holding a
baby wrapped in blankets and looking like, what
am I doing holding a baby? and he lifted this drain
cover by his foot in the road like he was going to
drop it down a drain into the sewer, but then he
decided against it, there was a policeman, and then
I was laughing too. There was all this laughing, the
wing was all the echo of them, and us, laughing.
Deets in here I've never seen laugh before or since,
deets I've never actually heard speak, the ones who
can't speak English and never say anything, the
violent ones. The fucked-up Iranian guy usually in
isolation, even he was laughing, everyone was, they
were like kids. He didn't drop the baby down the
drain, he took it home to a really minging poor
room, where everything was broken, and he
worked out how to feed it and keep it clean, and
then it grew into like a clever toddler who went
round throwing stones and breaking windows so
that the poor-guy character, who was kind of a
father to him, and who was a glass mender as a
job, could pass a broken window minutes after it
got broken with a new pane of glass on his back
and get paid by the housewife for mending it.*

*There was nothing to it, Britannia, stupid story
about a child, a man, a pane of glass, a stone, a
policeman. After it this place was like I've never*

seen. People in tears at the end of it. People wandered round the wing after it like we were all normal.

Sure it all descended pretty fast to the other normal again.

But I remember thinking it must've been a bit like it on the Christmas day in the trenches, remember in the video for the Paul McCartney Christmas song, when they played football with each other and gave each other their rations of smokes and their chocolate.

Here are some of the things Brittany Hall learned in her first two weeks as a DCO at a UK IRC:

- How to turn her body cam off until a deet was really about to lose his cool. *No point in filming something where someone's still calm*, the DCO called O'Hagan said. *Pigbollocks here, for example, is just holding forth right now, but you have to learn to sense when he'll get to about ten seconds off battering his head against the wall, and <u>then</u> you switch it on. You'll soon get the hang. No, he's fine. He's just kicking off. Nothing wrong with him. He's just doing it to annoy us.*

- How there was isolation for kicking off. No bedding, lights on 24/7, security checks every 15 mins 24/7.
- How one of the things you could say to deets on suicide watch was, *go on then, I dare you,* because mostly they were doing it to get attention or to annoy staff.
- How according to some DCOs *scrotum, pigbollocks, penis* and *prick* were all suitable things to call deets.
- How statistics had come back from an inspection visit saying that the deets liked the staff, found them on the whole approachable and reasonable. The statistic on this was particularly high from the deets who couldn't speak English.
- Which DCO was known as Officer Spice (the DCO called Brandon). He gave them what they wanted, what they really really wanted, and if there were any kids in, the kids were who Brandon or the deets got to test the spice to check it was any good.
- How there was generally paracetamol available for the Kurdish deet on the wing with cancer unless it was the weekend when no doctors were in, in which case he'd have to wait like everybody else for Monday.

- How management was thinking of putting a third bed in every room. Nobody working the wings thought this was a good idea. Staff had told management repeatedly it was a bad idea, Dave told her, but management was doing it anyway. *Not Three Men and a Baby, it's Three Men and a Toilet.* That was a reference to an old film. There were toilets in every room. *Ensuite. Ho ho ho.* The toilets had no lids and most of them were in the room with no screen or anything between them and the beds. This had a good knock-on effect of a lot of deets not eating much, given that nobody unless they're insane wants to shit in front of anyone else, and deets get locked in rooms for 13 hours 9pm till 8am and twice for roll call during the day, which Dave said was all good exercise for the sphincter.
- How the deets who'd been brought up in the UK were the most depressed and could be particularly troublesome, partly because none of the others would make friends with them. *I knew one*, Russell told her. *I saw him in here and I said to him, Laurie, man, what you doing in here? We'd been same class all through primary and secondary. Twelve years of school. He said, I got stop and*

searched outside a supermarket, I was
standing too close to a Porsche. They took
me into a station God knows where, then in
the middle of the night woke me up, put the
cuffs on and brought me here.

Next day I went into the office and I got
his notes looked up and he was about to be
deported to Ghana, literally next morning.
So I told him.

Ghana? he said. I don't know nothing
about Ghana. I never been to Ghana. I don't
even know where Ghana is.

• How Russell was all right but filthy minded,
crude as fuck. How Dave was all right. Torq
was all right. Torq liked books, a bit like Josh
except gay. He said in her ear on their first
shift together, as a famous writer put it in
the 1930s, cruelty to animals will get you
punished but cruelty to humans will get you
promotion. Was it advice? She wasn't sure
how to take it. She didn't know Torq well
enough at that point. She didn't yet know
what was funny and what wasn't. Someone
in the staffroom told a story like it was a joke
about the deet who'd been put on a plane before
he had a chance to find out that the papers
saying he could stay had arrived at the centre.
Was that funny? A lot of DCOs laughed.
Someone else told everyone this: okay, so a

deet makes a complaint to the HO. He says: I was in prison at home because they didn't like my politics. And prison at home is not that different from being in detention here in the UK, except that here in the UK I haven't been beaten up yet. So the HO writes back to him and says: happy to help (smiley face). Joke? Definitely meant to be. Big big laugh.

Where's Josh these days? what's the story with you and him? her mother'd said again at supper.

How should I know? Brit said.

Sorry I spoke, her mother'd said.

It was still September. Brit was on her bed in her bedroom now, getting some privacy.

The last time she'd seen Josh, in August, they'd gone to bed, rare enough now because of Josh's back but they had, good, then afterwards Josh had been going on and on about a history book he was reading where a man goes up to an SS guy in a city the Nazis have taken over and the SS guy has just clouted someone undesirable in the face with his pistol or something Nazi like that, and the man, a civilian, an old guy from a university or a school, professor type, goes to tell the SS guy to stop it, the words he actually uses are *have you no soul*. And the SS guy turns and shoots the professor in the head right then and there and the man falls down dead in the street.

Josh had started talking about it because she'd been telling him, before they got into bed, about how there was a deet called Hero in the centre and that sometimes names were really ironic. And when Josh said the stuff about the man that shot the learned man in the head, a darkness, but on the inside of her head, happened.

It came down over her eyes and forehead like a thick curtain, like old curtains from houses in past history or on Most Haunted on the Really channel, so real she could almost smell the curtain material.

Damp. Fust.

What I'm wondering is, Josh was saying. What the ethos is.

The what? she said.

Like, say in a Tarantino film, Josh said, when you see a man who's supposed to be a hard man turn on someone else like that and just shoot him dead it's pretty much supposed to be approved of, when it happens. Usually we're supposed to find it comedic.

Comedic, right, Brit said.

She and Josh had been top students in their year at school.

And we're supposed to think, Josh said, even if he's a bad cunt and a villain, that he's as cool as a hero because he's really hard. But. Does that mean the heroic *can* have no soul, I mean that someone with no soul can be heroic? And that we're supposed to think this is a good thing or a thing to aspire to?

Thing is, Josh, I can't really, don't really, give a fuck, Brit had said.

She'd turned over, away. She was knackered beyond belief. She had a headache from hell. There was a smell of rot in her nose. She closed her eyes. She opened them. There was dark inside and out.

You don't, do you? Josh had said. You can't.

He'd shunted himself out of bed.

I don't can't what? she said.

Give a fuck, he said. You said it. And it's true. You don't even really give a fuck when we're fucking any more. You can't give hardly anything. You've stopped giving.

Then they'd had the fight where he told her what she was doing with her life was the epitome of excrement. Josh liked to bandy big words about. Comedic, ethos, epitome, excrement.

How dare you speak to me like that? she said.

He laughed when she said that. His laughing made fury go furiously all through her.

What I'm saying is, you're only able to see things from the point of view of yourself, he said.

So? she said. That just makes me the same as everyone else living in the whole fucking world.

It's making you unreasoningly self-righteous, he

said. It's not your fault. You've taken a job that's making you go even more mad than the rest of us.

I've taken a job that's got a salary, she said. It's more than you're getting right now. It's definitely more than you got when you *were* working. It's a real job. Security delivers results.

(These were low blows. Josh had been laid off from the online delivery warehouse in May.)

Security, Josh said. That's what you call it. I call it upholding the illusion.

What illusion? she said.

That keeping people out is what it's all about, he said.

What *what's* all about? she said.

Being British, he said. English.

What the fuck are you on about? she said.

Wall ourselves in, he said. Shoot ourselves in the foot. Great nation. Great country.

It's you who's talking the epitome of excrement, she said. Political correct metropolitan liberal shit. Getting your opinions from the net and the papers. You're the fucking epitome of excrement yourself.

Why is that? Josh said.

He said it calmly. He was the kind of calm that made her angry. He was speaking like he was right and she was wrong.

No, really, Brittany, I mean it. Why am I excrement? he said. Tell me. Give me a reason. Just one good reason.

Because I say you are, she shouted.

See? Josh said still in the really calm way. That's what it's doing to you.

Slam. (Bedroom door.)

Brit pulled her clothes back on out on the landing, hoping his mother or father or brother weren't about to come up the stairs. Then she stood on the landing for a full minute and waited. But Josh didn't come out of his room to apologize.

Okay.

Whatever.

Slam. (Front door.)

Excrement, she thought all the way home, angry when she left his street, turning the corner into her own street angry, execrable fucking excrement, all over her hands at work again that day, and on her shoes, a fleck of it still on her ankle when she thought she'd got it all off.

One of the deets in constant watch had been throwing it. He did it all the time, to get attention.

It didn't matter how many times you washed your hands of it, or whether people cleaned it up or not. It was still everywhere.

I've done three years in here for the crime of being a migrant, a deet said to her. If you're keeping people here this long you may as well let us do something. We could take a degree. Do a useful thing.

Useful? she said. A degree? Ho ho ho.

I crossed the world to come here to ask you for help, a Kurdish deet said to her. And you locked me in this cell. Now I sleep every night in a toilet with some person I don't know whose religion I don't share.

It's a room, not a cell. And you're lucky you've got anywhere to sleep at all, she said.

One deet was lying on his back on the floor in his room with his head close to the toilet pan. He was staring from this angle upside down at something through the bars and the perspex high above his head.

Why can't we open window in this prison?
he said.

Open *a* window, she said, And this isn't a prison, it's a purpose-built Immigration Removal Centre with a prison design.

When you're live in Immigration Removal Centre with a prison design you dream air, the deet said.

When you're *living*, she said. Or, when you *live*. You dream *about* air.

Hero was his name. Vietnamese. His casenotes said he'd got here by being sealed in a haulage container for seven weeks.

A plane roared over.

Thank you for help with your language, Miss DCO B. Hall, he said. It is good to have help from people. Tell me. What is like to breath real air?

Breathe, she said. What *is it* like. Why are you lying on the floor? Counting the planes?

Planes shook the building at a rate of one every couple of minutes.

I watch clods, he said.

He meant clouds.

I *am watching*, she said. *Clouds*. To see if it's the shape of a horse? Or a map? I used to play that game.

He looked at her, then looked back up and away.

No horse. No map, he said.

That night she'd gone out with the girls on the staff plus Torq for a summer night of expensive drinking and tapas in Covent Garden. On the way from the tube she walked passed a couple caught in a traffic jam in a sports Audi with its roof down. They were screaming at each other.

It's all about you, the woman screamed at the man.

It's not all about me, the man screamed at the woman.

Brit had looked up. The sky above them all was cloudless. Clodless. She remembered from geography at school. Clouds could only form if they had a piece of something, like a tiny fragment of dust, or salt. Aerosol. The water vapour rises and sticks to it. Those great white shapes like the outbreaths of God in winter weather, or those little shreds of white, or the cloudbanks of dirty grey, were nothing but dust and water shaped by air. She was lying on her bed now looking at the Artex in

161

the ceiling. Artex was asbestos. Her father had died of complications from asbestosis and there it was in all their fucking ceilings.

Never mind.

September now.

All the hot summer, people everywhere had been bright red with rage, near purple with rage.

It's all about you.

Now it was cooler, she was cooler too about it all. She was learning how to clod, ho ho. Easy as this: she switched the light off. She placed the spare pillow over her head.

She slept. Night passed. The phone alarm went off. She woke up.

She got up, put clean clothes on, got the bus to the station to get the train to work.

One day some BBC people were outside the overground. They were asking people things for something about today. A man put a long mic under her nose. Another man said to her, *tell us what Brexit means to you.*

She thought about all the people in the centre.

She thought about Stel from Welfare telling her how much harder it was to get anyone to listen to anything welfare-based about deets, out of sight and mind now that everyone from everywhere else was an immigrant too and legal immigrants were just as unpopular with the media and the general public as illegals.

Just get on with it, right? she said into the mic.

The interviewer nodded like what she said mattered.

You think the government should just get on with it, he said.

Yeah, she said. What choice we got? To be honest, it means fuck all now. Excuse my English. I mean there's a world out there bigger than Brexit, yeah? But. Whatever.

The interviewer asked her what she'd voted in the EU Referendum.

No, see, I'm not going to tell you what I voted. I'm not going to let you think you can decide something about me either way. All I'll say is, I was younger then, and I still thought politics mattered. But all this. This endless. It's eating the, the, you know. Soul. Doesn't matter what I voted or you voted or anyone voted. Because what's the point, if nobody in the end is going to listen to or care about what other people think unless they think and believe the same thing as them. And you people. Asking us what we think all the time like it matters. You don't care what we think. You just want a fight. You just want us to fill your air. Tell you what it's doing. It's making us all meaningless. You're making us meaningless, and the people in power, doing it all for *us*, for *democracy*, yeah, right, pull the other one. They're doing it for their pay-off. They make us more meaningless every day.

They thanked her. They asked her her name and what she did for a living.

Brittany Hall. I'm a DCO at an IRC.

The female assistant wrote it down without asking what it was. She wrote it down like the Britney in Britney Spears. People are often careless like that. She wrote it all down wrong. Britney Hall DC RC.

So it didn't really matter, then, what or who Brit was.

She went through the barrier, got on the train (no seats left now because they'd wasted her time) and went to work.

She got off the train. She walked down the road from the station between the airport fencing rolls of razor wire and through the management/visitor car park.

Hello, hedges.

Here are some of the things Brittany Hall learned in her first two months as a DCO at a UK IRC:

- What privacy meant. (It meant she wasn't a deet.)
- What effect an official report about an independent inspection of the centre had on the place: it meant there was a new water cooler installed in the visits room.
- How there were 30,000 people detained in this country at any one time, and that was the level of interned deets across detention estate that kept SA4A salaries stable.
- How the deets wandered the wings like they were jetlagged. They got more jetlagged the

longer they were detained. They'd arrive for the first time and make friends with the people they'd something in common with, place of origin, religion, language. Then that friendship just died, you saw it time and time again, because what they really now had in common was shit, an open toilet, and being stuck in here in indefinite detention, which means no way of knowing when you'll be out of here or if you ever will, and if you are, how long it'll be before you're right back in again.

- How to choose which deets to speak to, who to ignore.
- How to talk weather with other DCOs while they're holding someone in headlock or four of you are sitting on someone to calm him.
- How to say without thinking much about it, *they're kicking off. We're not a hotel. If you don't like it here go home. How dare you ask for a blanket.* The day she heard herself say that last one she knew something terrible was happening, but by now the terrible thing, as terrible as a death, felt quite far away, as if not really happening to her, as if happening beyond perspex, like the stuff in the windows in the centre, which weren't really windows, though they were designed to look like windows.

Detention is the key to maintaining an effective immigration system

HO

Nobody is detained indefinitely and regular reviews of detention are undertaken to ensure that it remains lawful and proportionate

HO HO HO

Then this happened.

It was a Monday in October. Brit got off the train. It was mid-morning. She was on the pm shift. She walked down the stairs to the barriers and out.

A schoolkid was sitting on one of the metal seats outside the station.

Excuse me, the kid said.

Me? Brit said.

(There were quite a few people who'd just got off the train.)

Could you help me with something, please? the girl said.

Brit looked at her phone to check the time.

Shouldn't someone your age be in school? she said.

That is actually a really good question, the girl said.

Better answer it then, Brit said.

I will, the girl said. In good time. But right now I'm wondering.

Wondering what? Brit said.

What DCO means, the girl said.

What? Brit said. Oh.

(The girl was at eye level with Brit's lanyard.)

It means I'm a Custody Officer, Brit said.

What's the D for? the girl said.

Detainee, Brit said.

What's the B for? the girl said.

Brit caught her lanyard up in her hand.

That's my first name, Brit said.

Your first name's just the letter B? the girl said. That is so cool. That is such a good idea.

Don't be stupid, Brit said. It's the first letter of my name, obviously.

I'm going to change my name just to its first letter, the girl said.

What's your first name? Brit said.

F, the girl said.

That made Brit laugh out loud.

What's it really? she said.

Florence, the girl said.

Well, if you're Florence, does that make me the machine? Brit said.

The girl looked delighted. Brit felt weirdly elated to have delighted anyone.

Come on. People must make that joke at you all the time with a name like Florence, Brit said.

They do. But usually they say, where's your machine, Florence, or something like that.
Nobody's actually declared themselves my machine before, the girl said.

Yeah, but I really am the machine, Brit said. And not necessarily your machine. And right now the word the machine is saying to you is: school. Shouldn't you be working hard learning equations or something? What school do you go to? I mean, not go to?

That made the girl laugh too. Brit tried to read the little coat of arms on the laughing girl's blazer. Vivunt spe. Latin. Living, live. They are living. Something.

The girl got something out of her pocket and held it out to Brit to take. Brit sat down on the metal seat next to her.

It was a postcard, an old-looking one, like one that'd been sent years ago, of a low stony river and some trees. Three kids in the picture were paddling quite far away in it in river water which was a bright blue. Its blue had been enhanced, it was fake, the water wasn't really that blue; maybe the green had been greened up too. But it was a sunny day in the postcard, with a hazed blue sky, a single cloud, hilly slopes and mountains in the distance, some trees, a stony bank down to the river, a lot of grass behind. At the bottom of the card it said KINGUSSIE · The River Gynack and

Golf Course 5359W and when you knew that a golf course was what it was, you could also make out three very small people in the far distance of the picture, presumably golfers.

Uh huh, Brit said. Who's it from? Can I read the back, or is it private?

Yif, the girl said.

Yif? What's yif mean? Brit said.

Yif means yes if you want, the girl said.

Thill, Brit said.

What's thill mean? the girl said.

Thanks, I will, Brit said.

You speak my language! the girl said.

It *was* old, postmarked decades ago, a decade before Brit had even been born:

5.30pm 16 04 86 INVERNESS A 'Hail Caledonia' Product Dear Simon we arrived in Kingussie Saturday night 5.30 It was a nice journey. The weather here is very warm with plenty of sun today Monday I am going to Inverness in the afternoon to have a look at Loch Ness by coach so cheerio now. From Uncle Desmond

She gave it back to the girl.

And? she said.

Where is this place on the card, exactly? the girl said.

Tells you its name, right there, Brit said.

Where in the country? the girl says.

Look it up, Brit said. Look it up on a phone or a computer. If you were in school right now, you could do it really easily.

What if I don't want to use a computer? the girl said.

Because? Brit said.

I just don't, the girl said.

Because? Brit said.

I want to travel with no footprint, the girl said.

Because? Brit said.

That's right, the girl said. Because.

Why would anyone want to do that? Brit said.

You should know, the girl said. You're the machine. But how do I get to it? I mean really. Is it in this country?

You'll have to ask your parents, Brit said.

Let's assume, let's just assume, the girl said. That I don't want to ask anyone.

Why not? Brit said.

Except you, the girl said.

You're asking the machine, Brit said.

No, I'm asking you, the girl said. What do I do?

Well, it's in Scotland, Brit said.

Is it? the girl said. Wow.

Yes, Brit said. (99.99% sure; at first she'd thought it might be Devon from the strangeness of the

173

name, or if not maybe Yorkshire. But Loch Ness it said on the back. Loch Ness was definitely Scotland.)

Where is it, I mean from here? the girl said. I mean I know where Scotland is. But where in Scotland? How does a person go to this place?

A person can fly, or take a train, or a bus is probably cheapest, Brit said. A person needs an adult to buy that person a ticket, most probably. If a person wants to spend money a person could probably get a flight from here to somewhere reasonably near. Is it specifically this river the person wants to get to? Course it is. I can see. You're clearly a big golfer. Doing the rounds of the rounds, doing a tour of all the golf courses in the country. I can always spot a golfer.

The girl went molten next to her with laughter.

How's your birdie? I mean your eagle. How's your bogey? Brit said.

They're all fine thank you, the girl said.

You'll have to be careful not to hit the ball into the water of the river whatsitsname, Brit said. Show me again. Gynack. Sounds a bit medical. What about Uncle Desmond? Is he a golfer? What about Simon? Have they got a car? They could drive you there.

I don't know them, the girl said. I think they're not relevant.

Not relevant? Nobody's not relevant, Brit said.

I will hold you to that statement, the girl said.

What I mean is, I think the card is just an example, and all that I need to take from it is the name of the place I've to get to.

So who sent you the card, then? Brit said. Could they drive you there? How about your family?

What if someone doesn't have a family to drive her in a car? the girl said.

How do you mean, doesn't have a family? Brit said.

Have you got a car? the girl said.

Would I be taking this train to work every day if I had a car? Brit said.

You might be, if you were environmentally minded, the girl said. Would you drive me to this place?

It's the people who look after you who should take you, not someone you don't know, Brit said. You can't just ask strangers to drive you up and down the country. This is the twenty first century. Strangers are more dangerous than ever; we've never been more dangerous. Who looks after you?

Foster family, the girl said.

And where do the Foster family live? Brit said.

Then she said, oh. Foster family.

I have to get to here, the girl said. It is imperative. Soon as possible.

Your foster family'll take you, Brit said.

The girl shook her head.

Why do you want to go there so much? Brit said.

What's happening there? Can't be that urgent.
Posted more than thirty years ago, ha ha.

To go there on a train, the girl said. Which
station would you go to in London to get to it from?

Ask your foster mum. Get her to look it up on her
phone, Brit said.

Can you look it up for me on *your* phone? the
girl said.

Uh, Brit said. How about. If I do, will you do
something for me?

I might, the girl said.

Deal, Brit said. Or clearly as much of a deal as
I'm going to get.

She got her phone out. She saw how late for work
she was. But she typed the name of the place in and
held it up for the girl to see.

Trains every day from here direct, Brit said.
Or – you could go to *this* place, which is the . . .
the what?

She put her finger on the word Edinburgh and
showed the girl.

Capital of? Brit said.

Are all machines this patronizing? the girl said.

That's machine nature for you, Brit said. Which
reminds me. I've got work. Okay, so you get to
there, and you change to another train to get to
there.

If we went today, the girl said. Could we get there
today?

If you went today, uh, I don't know, Brit said. I'd say probably not. Not on a train. On a plane, yes. It's pretty far north.

Oh.

The girl's face fell.

You could probably get part of the way there in one day and do the rest the next, Brit said. But I better not be aiding and abetting a runaway telling you all this. You better not be running away.

It is not in my nature to run away from anything, the girl said.

Good. Right then, Brit said. You owe me.

Owe you what? the girl said.

I did something for you, Brit said. You promised you'd do something for me.

What I said was, I might, the girl said.

I want you to promise me, Brit said, that you'll phone and tell the people who look after you where you are and what it is you're thinking of doing.

Can't, the girl said.

Why not? Brit said.

Don't have a phone, the girl said.

She was up and off running towards the front of the station.

Tell me their names and a number for them, so I can let them know where you are, Brit called after her. Tell me the name of your school. At least.

Come on! the girl said. Quick. We'll miss it.

I can't go anywhere with you, Brit said.

She heard the girl tell the man who looked after the barriers that she didn't have a ticket. The man opened the barriers anyway. She heard the girl say a flying thank you. She got her phone back out to dial – to dial what? Who? 999? Fire? Police? Ambulance?

When she looked up from her screen the girl had disappeared up towards the platforms.

She shook her head. She turned to go on down the road to work.

Three minutes down the airport road she stopped. She turned on her heels.

She ran back up to the station. She stood at the closed barriers.

Let me through, quick, will you? she called to the man who operated the barriers.

He came over.

Ticket? he said.

I just want to catch that kid up that you let through a minute ago, she said.

You'll need a valid ticket, the man said.

Long long ago in the morning of what was actually still today, Brit had been on her way to work. But now, opposite her on a train speeding its way up the map of England, the girl, Florence, is talking about the invisible life she says there is in *this* –

she is pointing at a spill of water out of one of the water bottles on the table between them

– so he got the idea for the first microscopes, she is saying. He was something to do with the making of cloth and he wanted to be able to see what the threads he was making his cloth with looked like really close up. So he taught himself to grind glass out of sand, which is how you make glass.

No. Is it? Brit said.

Yeah, it really is, the girl says, and he ground it into exceptionally small but powerful lenses so he could look at things magnified hundreds and hundreds of times.

Exceptionally, Brit says.

Then he invented a wooden thing to hold the lenses up to your eye, the girl says, it was only this size, literally, because the lenses were so small too, but though his lenses were quite definitely tiny the human eye could still look through them and perceive the small things made massive.

Perceive, Brit says. Big word.

My mother always says as a general rule it's a good thing to make the world bigger, not smaller, the girl says. And then the Dutchman thought, great, I can look at all sorts of things really close up now, and one day in the year 1670-something he was eating his lunch and there was pepper sprinkled on it. And he thought to himself, I bet if I look at a grain of pepper through one of my lenses that the grain of pepper will have sharp sides, or lots of prickles on it like a hedgehog, because that's what it feels like on my tongue, like it's pricking it with invisible pointed sticks. So he soaked some grains of pepper in water for like a month. And then he looked at the pepper-water through a lens that made it 200 times closer than the naked eye can see. And he saw that the water was filled with little, animalcules is the word he called them, like the word molecules, all swimming about. So he tried looking again, this time with water that didn't have any pepper in it, and the animalcules were still there in it so that meant it wasn't the pepper that put them there.

And there's this other really cool thing he did. He used one of his lenses to look through the eye of a dragonfly. He cut into a dragonfly eye, the dragonfly was already dead –

How d'you know for sure? Brit says.

– don't be horrible, and he took out a piece of its eye and placed it on one of his lenses. And when he looked through them both at once out of his window, the lens and the piece of dragonfly eye, he saw his own street, but like an app effect of his own street, with the same picture repeating from different angles a lot of times so it becomes dimension, and that's how we know what some insects' eyes can see and how.

And one of the other things he looked at was at the bacteria off his own teeth. And at rainwater. And he looked at the oil out of coffee beans, and at frogspawn, and, and anyway now we know what microbes are and what cells are and that the naked human eye can only see a fraction of what is actually there. And that this –

(the spill of water on the table)

– is full of life we can't see, and just because we can't see it doesn't mean it isn't. It really really is. And if you look at, say, a pine needle, just a pine needle, a single needle out of the millions that grow

on just one tree in just one pine wood, if you cut
into a single one and magnify a fraction of it so you
can look at its structure really close up, it looks like
a painting or like stained glass, or a mosaic by
ancient Romans or the wings of a butterfly, and you
can see it's got a cellular structure, and that pine
needles are really cleverly designed so that they can
make sunlight into nourishment when it's winter,
and hold on to enough moisture in the hot months
of summer. And that's how they stay green.

Basic biology. Stuff Brit knows already, or knew
but has forgotten since school, where you have to
know that kind of stuff to pass. But Brit is listening
to the girl tell her it, sitting in the low flash of
afternoon sun coming through the break in the
cloud and hitting the train window between
telegraph poles like a drumbeat, hitting Brit like
she's being played by light.

Truth be told, if Brit could thumb back through
all the weeks of her time on earth so far, every one
of its Mondays, she'd still end up 100% sure that
she's never been happier on a Monday afternoon
than she is right now.

She is on a train with a child who's nothing
to do with her, going God knows where, God
knows why.

She is not at work where she monitors indefinitely
interned humans for a salary –

because looking is just the start of understanding,

just its surface, the top layer of any understanding, the girl is saying

– and for sure it's a long long time since Brit has even allowed herself to remember the more-than-one meaning in a word like cell. Strange, given that she works in a building full of them.

She'd got on the Edinburgh train at King's Cross at the back and walked up the carriages watching out for the child. Five carriages in she'd spotted her sitting by herself at a table seat pulling her school shirt sleeves down inside her blazer sleeves.

The train slipped out into suburbs and open country and Brit stood in the space between the carriages masked by people's luggage, keeping an eye on the girl through the glass of the door and holding her phone with the work number up on it.

She pressed call. Recep answered. She stepped back round the corner and asked to be put through to Stel.

They put her through to Stel's office answerphone, where anyone in the office might hear her message as she was leaving it.

So she hung up and called Stel's mobile. It put her through to its answerphone. Hi, she said, Stel, it's Brit Hall here, listen. I'm on a train with the girl, you know that girl who got them to clean the place up last month? I think it's her. I'm pretty sure it's her. So I'm on this train, and she's on the same train, I can see her from here, and I, uh, I –

183

She held her phone away from herself.

Train noise will have recorded itself on Stel's answerphone for those few seconds.

She pressed 1.

The answerphone voice told her she could press 2 to re-record her message. She pressed 2. She held the phone in the train air and let it record that air over the track laid down by her own voice.

Then she put her phone back in her coat pocket and stepped on the place which makes the door slide open.

The girl looked up from a school notebook she had open in front of her.

Kept you a seat, she said. And furthermore.

She said it like they were still mid-conversation, like they hadn't been in different trains crossing London separately for the last couple of hours.

If the force of just five more nuclear bombs going off anywhere in the world happens, she said, an eternal nuclear autumn will set in and there'll be no more seasons.

Who taught you that paranoid rubbish? Brit said.

It's not rubbish. It's a bona fide warning for the future, the girl said. Don't you know about how hot the seas are? If you don't you can find it on the net. You can just look it up. It's your future too as well as mine.

I thought you didn't like using the net, Brit said.

I choose only to use it wisely, the girl said.

Who died and made you the new Socrates? Brit said.

I think if you're talking classically you might mean the new Cassandra, the girl said.

Think you're clever, Brit said.

Hope I am, the girl said. Clever enough. Hope you are too.

Oh, I'm plenty clever, thanks, Brit said.

Intelligent machine, the girl said.

That's me, Brit said, sitting down in the seat the girl had kept for her.

There is a woman sitting at the table across the aisle from them who looked horrified when the girl said that the spill of water on the table was full of life.

There are people on the train all round them looking at screens, holding screens up to their ears and noses, holding them in their laps.

Instead, she and the girl have spent the last while playing what the girl calls Lucky 13.

The game is, I ask thirteen questions, then we both have to answer them. Right? the girl said.

Right, Brit said.

What's your favourite colour, song, food, drink, thing to wear, place, season, day of the week. What animal would you be if you were an animal. What bird. What insect. What one thing are you really good at. How would you most like to die.

Oh, that last question's a bloody depressing question, Brit said. Who invented this game?

I did, the girl said. And that last question's precisely why the word lucky's in the title of the game.

What's lucky about having a favourite way to die? Brit said.

If you don't know how lucky you are to be even discussing the chance of a choice, the girl said, then all I can say is, you're really really lucky.

Here are the girl's answers:

Favourite colour turquoise.

Favourite two songs Self by No Name (Brit's never heard of No Name, but she's not exactly got time to be up on the music scene these days) and Ooh Child by Nina someone (Brit doesn't know that one either).

Favourite food pizza.

Favourite drink orange juice at breakfast time.

Favourite thing to wear the jeans embroidered with flowers she got for her birthday this year.

Favourite place home.

Favourite season spring.

Favourite day of the week Friday.

If she was an animal she'd be a pink fairy armadillo (apparently there is such a thing).

If she was a bird she'd be one of the robins that
  sing in the middle of the night in December.
If she was an insect she'd be a dragonfly
  because of what she knows about their eyes.
The penultimate question is a trick question,
  she says, because most people are good at
  way more than just the one thing and this is
  supposed to get them thinking about it.
And she would most like to die before anybody
  else that she loves, so she won't have to
  miss them.

The woman opposite them starts clipping her
fingernails with a little clipper, like the train is her
private bedroom or bathroom.

Someone else is talking so loud on a phone it's
like the train's his private office.

The girl thumbs through the notebook she was
reading when Brit sat down. Hot Air, it says in
Sharpie in capitals on the cover. A geography
project, maybe science. Convection. She is writing
something down in it and singing an old folk song
to herself. Brit leans back in the seat and she hears,
with her eyes closed, the clip of the nails, the voice
of the man, and underneath both the girl singing
the old song. Fresh are the roses culled from the
garden, oh don't deceive me, oh never leave me.
Are they still teaching kids that old song at school?
Such a happy sounding song about deception.

I suppose it's because the person singing it isn't actually the maiden who's been done over, she thinks.

But pink fairy armadillo.

Dragonfly.

Bird singing in December.

There is no way this is the same child people were saying walked into – and untouched out of – a really nasty sex house in Woolwich.

Here's the first of my Lucky 13 for you, Brit says. Question 1. Tell me about your family.

No, the girl says. Next question.

Your mother, Brit says. Tell me something about her. Or your father.

That's private, the girl says. But I can tell you something that's nothing to do with all that.

What? Brit says.

When I was on that last train to King's Cross there was a boy opposite me with his mates and he was reading out emojis off his phone, and he said this:

Loveheart loveheart loveheart.

Loveheart loveheart.

Loveheart.

Loveheart.

My next question, then, Brit said. Got a boyfriend?

Private private private, the girl says. Private private. Private. Private. You?

Maybe, Brit says. What about your brothers or sisters?

That's private, the girl says. You?

Only child, Brit says. That thing your mother said, about the big and the small, it's really helpful. It's really well said. Tell me another good thing your mother says about life.

Uh-uh, the girl says.

Yeah, my family life's private too, Brit says. But how do we get to be friends, or even know each other at all, without you telling me a bit about what your life's like and me swapping with you what mine is like?

Making friends with a machine, the girl says. No way. It's quicksand.

Wait, I've an idea, Brit says. How about: I make up a story about someone, a member of my family. Then you do it too for one of yours. I'll tell you the story of why my mother called me Brittany.

Brittany like the place? the girl says.

Yep, Brit says. But everybody calls me Brit.

I'm a place too, the girl says. City in Italy. You're actually almost more than one place. You're nearly two different places. Britain and Brittany.

That's because – uh – my mother, get this, I'm not lying, is a geography textbook, Brit says. Don't laugh. It's true. My mother spent a lot of her early life in a school cupboard. She was in there for ages, longing for the cupboard to be opened. She was desperate to be opened herself, too, and read, especially by someone who loved what she'd tell them, someone who'd learn things from all the facts she had in her about the world. She was bursting with maps, with placenames and the coordinates of countries and cities, and things about trees, and cloud formations, she could hardly contain all her facts and figures about rivers, valleys, mountains, plains, seas, erosion, all that.

Is she not a geography book any more, then? the girl says.

Brit thinks of her mother at home right now.

24-hour news channel. *Wonder what'll happen.*

She's retired now, she says. She's, uh, a bit outdated, as texts go.

It seems a shame, the girl says. Your story's kind of a tragedy.

It is, Brit says.

As she says it she realizes she is finding it hard not to be moved to tears herself by her own ridiculous story about her mother.

She widens her eyes to stop herself.

She is also feeling a kind of shame. Her mother, a silly story. Her mother with all her complex shifts of colour through her face and neck whenever she feels anything. Her mother with all the maddening habits that Brit knows aren't maddening at all, are just maddening to Brit because Brit's her daughter.

The very thought of her mother as a book open

in someone's hands, held with kindness, makes Brit want to cry.

How did she get out of the cupboard in the first place? the girl is saying. How does a book give birth? How did a book give birth to *you*? Why aren't you a book? What about your father? Was he another geography book? Was he a different kind of book, a history book? Maths? Poetry? What does that make you?

No, it's your turn now, Brit says. To tell me a story about someone. How about a mother. I told you about mine. It doesn't have to be your own mother. Just any mother will do.

The girl shakes her head.

My story is lost at sea, she says. The end.

Your mother? Brit says.

The girl looks at her dolefully.

Your father? Brit says.

The girl looks at her dolefully.

That's terrible, Brit says.

The girl looks at her dolefully.

Is it true? Brit says.

True to what you want to hear me say, the girl says. But the real story is, I'm not going to tell you anything. You can sit in the comfy plastic body-moulded armchair with integrated drinking hole for your Coke in the warm multiscreen cineplex of your own preconception for as long as you like, and think what you like while you do.

Wow, Brit says. You're off the scale. Where did you learn to talk like that?

Your turn again, the girl says. Go on. Surprise *my* preconceptions.

Yeah, but your story was way too short, Brit says.

It's a short story, the girl says.

Then Brit and the girl move to a two-seater so a couple and their kids can all sit together; the family gets off at Newcastle and the train quietens down again. A ticket inspector comes through the carriage. He tells Brit he won't fine her this time but not to do it again. He asks her where she got on. He lets her buy a ticket at an unpenalized rate with her card and he gives her a smile as he leaves.

He doesn't even look at the girl, never mind ask whether she's got a ticket or who's going to pay for it.

Brit raises her eyebrows at the girl when she hears the door swish shut behind him.

Smooth move, Florence, she says.

I didn't do anything, the girl says.

Have you actually got a ticket? Brit says.

Sometimes I am invisible, the girl says. In certain shops or restaurants or ticket queues or supermarkets, or even places when I'm actually speaking out loud, like asking for information in a station or something. People can look right through me. Certain white people in particular can look right through young people and also black and mixed race people like we aren't here.

That'd explain how you got into our boss's office last month, Brit says.

It is strangely easy to bring it up now that they're both facing the same way. When the girl was sitting opposite her something had stopped Brit from asking. But now that they're both not looking directly at each other, both looking ahead, she's able to say outright,

it was you, yeah?

The girl turns away to the window humming an old song again, Ash Grove this time, flicking through her notebook.

It explains how you got past recep, that's what we call reception, and through the scans, Brit says. Which is not supposed to be humanly possible. But now I get it. You were invisible.

The girl looks out the window.

What I want to know most is this, Brit says. We all want to know this. I mean all of us at work. Because there's a lot we'd like to say to him, and we never get the chance. What did you say to him?

The girl keeps her back turned towards Brit. She says nothing.

Well, I don't know if you know this, Brit says. But whatever it was you said to him. It meant they really cleaned the place up. They brought cleaners in that evening and they steamcleaned the toilets.

It was quite a day, that day, after they cleaned up in there, Brit says. There's only ever been another day like it in the centre, according to my friend Torquil, when all the people, staff included, were so, uh, I can't think of the word.

Clean, the girl says.

Yeah, Brit says.

Is that all they did, the girl says without turning round. Clean the toilets up.

She says it like it's not a question. But Brit is now 99.99% certain she is on a train with the girl who outwitted the system.

She plays it calm. She changes the subject. She taps the school notebook in the girl's hand.

Hot Air, Brit says. School thing.

Not directly, the girl says. This is for what my, someone I know, gave me, because I sometimes have ideas and they thought I should write them down.

The girl shows Brit, but only for a fraction of a second, a flash of the inside front page, at the top of which, under the underlined words Your Hot Air Book, someone has written the words RISE MY DAUGHTER ABOVE, with some lines of handwriting beneath.

Can I look a bit more slowly at it? Brit says.

No, the girl says.

What else is written in it? Brit says.

Hot air, the girl says. Private hot air.

A voice announces over the loudspeaker system that they're soon to arrive in the place called Berwick-upon-Tweed.

Scotland any minute, Brit says.

But I don't have a passport, the girl says.

You don't need one, Brit says. Not for this border. Not yet, anyway.

How do you mean not yet? the girls says.

Well, Scotland and England, Brit says. Goes without saying.

What does? the girl says.

Different countries, Brit says.

Will we be able to see it? the girl says.

Scotland? Brit says.

The difference, the girl says.

She jams herself against the window.

Actually I think we may already be in Scotland, Brit says.

I didn't see any border, the girl says. Did you see it? I don't see anything different.

There was a time in history, Brit says, when passports didn't exist at all, for anywhere. People could go anywhere. It's not actually that long ago.

Did your father the history book tell you that? the girl says.

My father, Brit says. A history book. When I tell my mother that. She'll laugh like a drain.

The girl turns in her seat and starts to talk.

If, instead of saying, like, this border divides

these places, we said something like – like about your mother being a geography book – what about if we said, my mother is two different countries and my father is a border.

You'd never get away with that, Brit says. Mothers would really complain they were being blocked off. Fathers would declare they were going to expand till they became the size of both the countries on either side of them. Whole new kinds of divorce proceedings would take place.

Are *your* parents divorced? the girl says.

That's private, Brit says.

What if, the girl says. Instead of saying, this border divides these places. We said, this border *unites* these places. This border holds together these two really interesting different places. What if we declared border crossings places where, listen, when you crossed them, you yourself became doubly possible.

You're being naive, Brit says. In so many ways.

I'm twelve, the girl says. What do you expect? But listen. Just say. Say. Instead of having to prove who you are with a paper booklet or by showing a screen your eye or the print in your finger or the information about your face. Instead, you could prove who you are by what you *see* with your eyes and by what you *make* with your hands and –

And by the faces you can make with your face,

Brit says. There'd be all-out war. The Tongue-Roll wars would happen.

What are the Tongue-Roll wars? the girl says.

The wars against people who can roll their tongues due to a genetic disposition, Brit says. Attacked by the people who genetically can't. And/ or vice versa. One way or another there'd be war. Can you roll your tongue?

The girl tries. Brit laughs, and shows her.

Yeah, but you being able to do it and me not being able to doesn't make me want to go to war with you, the girl says.

Believe me, Brit says. It can come down to something as genetically random as that.

What can? the girl says.

Hatred, Brit says.

The girl sighs.

Brittany, you are vetoing all my imaginative plans, she says.

Course I am, Brit says.

It isn't fair, the girl says.

That's correct, Brit says.

You are being pessimistic, the girl says.

I'm being truthful, Brit says.

Inhuman, the girl says.

It's my job, Brit says.

We can change your job, the girl says.

Can't teach an old machine new tricks, Brit says.

Built-in obsolescence, the girl says. You'll

rust. But don't worry, because when you do, we'll oil you and adapt you and upgrade you to a new way of working.

We'll see about that, Brit says.

We'll see, we'll see, with any luck like dragonflies from all the angles, the girl says. We'll begin again. We'll revolve.

You mean we'll evolve, Brit says.

No, I mean revolve, the girl says. As in revolution. We'll roll forward to a new place.

You mean revolt, Brit says. You're talking about revolting.

I mean revolve, the girl says.

No you don't, Brit says.

I do. We'll turn it round, the girl says. We'll do it all differently.

She turns her back on Brit in her seat, turns back to the window and stares out into the dark like she's trying to make out what some far lights are.

It's not long after this that the girl falls asleep, just falls asleep in a moment, like a young cat or young dog might, with a sleep that simply stops her, drops her into it, against Brit, on a train going through the darkness in a whole other country, somewhere Brit knew existed but she's never been.

I mean, look at Brittany Hall.

She literally can't believe her own life.

She is clever again.

She is witty and entertaining.

She is on the ball, too.

She should be at work. It's a Monday.

Instead, no hedges, no underworld, here she is, and a child – not just any child, but a real child who also happens to be the *legendary* child – is not just sitting next to her but has fallen so completely asleep against her right arm that Brit feels more protective about somebody she doesn't know, no relation, some stranger's child she only met this morning, than she knew she could feel about anyone or anything.

She reaches round and slides the Hot Air book out from under the girl's arm. She opens it one-handedly, flicks through it.

It is full of little written pieces in schoolgirl handwriting, like little stories.

One is in the voice of lots of websites and social media sites. It is actually really funny and sharp. Brit has to stop herself shaking with laughing and waking the girl.

One is like a lot of the far right and far left stuff that people say, and the girl has written it all in different sizes of writing, some bits in capitals. Though it's naive, the kind of stuff a school student would write, it's witty too, and it makes Brit think.

Even a twelve-year-old girl can see through a lot of what's happening in the world right now.

There's a paragraph written like a wall, of the obscene kinds of twitter language. Then there's a really good story, like a fairy story, about a girl who refuses to dance herself to death even though a whole villageful of people and millions of people online want her to.

She closes the book and puts it on top of the girl's schoolbag. Pink.

Brit's own favourite colour is blue.

Her favourite song is Heroes by Alesso (though she also likes the Adele song When We Were Young because it reminds her of Josh and her, back when they were at school, back before Josh's back went).

Her favourite food is anything burnt or covered in barbecue sauce.

Her favourite drink is vodka.

Her favourite thing to wear is nothing at all (but she wouldn't say such a thing to a child, she talked about her little blue All Saints dress instead), her favourite place is Florida where she and her mum and her dad went on holiday when she was ten, her favourite season is winter, her favourite day of the week is Friday, if she was an animal she'd be a lioness, bird a kestrel, insect something that can eat spiders.

Thing she's good at? inventing things.

Fave way to die? in bed asleep knowing nothing whatsoever about it.

The battery charger in your trainers so that you charge things while you just walk around is a brilliant invention idea, the girl had said. Someone should make those right now and sell them. You should leave your job and make those. Also, we both like the same day best. And. If we were seasons, I would be following you.

You'd be the end of me, Brit said. You'd kill me off.

No, you'd make me be possible, the girl now leaning against her fast asleep had said.

Then all afternoon on the train, whenever anybody went past wearing blue the girl nudged her and said the word blue.

Who has given a fuck about Brit's favourite anything for more than ten seconds in the last ten years?

It is like being in a fairy tale herself.

She should text her mother. *I'm in an effing fairy tale. Wonder what will happen.*

It feels a little dangerous, to be so close to fairy tale.

What role is she meant to be playing? Is she older and wiser and there to give advice?

Is she magic? Or in need of magic? Is she jealous? Is she enchanted? Is she lost in the wood, young and foolish and about to learn a lesson? Is she the guardian of something really precious?

Is she wicked, or good?

She looks out into the darkness, seeing nothing but her own face.

(She'll be surprised, on the way back down south

in a couple of days, when she sees a sea out there which on the way up she'd absolutely no idea was there.)

Somebody somewhere will be worrying themselves sick about where this child is.

She will try to find out who to tell.

Plus, when they hear about this at work nobody will believe it.

Plus, she is definitely tailing the girl's parents now, or at least one of them.

There may be promotion in it.

She gets her phone out of her pocket as carefully as she can so as not to disturb the sleeping girl.

She texts Josh for the first time since the summer fight.

Hey Josh its me i have some latin translation for you text me back tell me what does it mean vivunt spe

What SA4A IRC Manager Bernard Oates and
Florence Smith said to each other that day in
September:

– Hi.

– What the f –

– I'm here today to ask you some questions.

– You're what?

– So. Firstly. My first question is.

– Who are you?

– Why are all the toilets for the people who are
being detained by you in here so dirty?

– The –? (Calling) Sandra! Sandra, can you come
in here a moment?

– Okay, so what I plan to do is, when you can't
or don't answer a question I ask, I won't bother you
with it again, I'll just go on to the next question.
So, my next question is: Why do you handcuff the

people who come here when they're being brought here or taken out of here, when they aren't actually criminals?

– Did Graham put you in here? Did he, did they, who told you to ask me about toilets?

– Okay, thanks. Next question is two questions. Why, when you bring people here, do you bring them in the middle of the night? And why do you use vans whose windows are blacked out when it's dark in the middle of the night anyway?

– Was it Evie in Personnel? Did Evie put you up to this?

– Okay, so we'll go to my next question, which is this. Why do the doors on the rooms here have no handles on the inside?

– How do you – Are you in the family unit? You can't do a school thing here. You can't do a project about here. This is a restricted area.

– Okay. Why is it the Prison and Probation department and the people who work for it who are dealing with people who are refugees and have come to this country from other countries they can't stay in because of things like being tortured or wars or not having enough to eat?

– Stop asking these, these. What are you writing down?

– Mr Oates, did you know you're breaking the law? It says in law that you can only legally detain someone in this country for seventy

two hours before you have to charge them with
a crime.

– You're not allowed. It's not allowed, you need
clearance, you're not permitted to be –

– The other thing I wanted to ask is. I read online
yesterday that the High Court has said it's also
illegal to detain, in detention centres like this one,
people who have been tortured. And then I read
that the Home Office redefined the word torture to
give it a more 'narrow' definition. So I wanted to
ask someone who might know. What is a narrow
definition of torture and what is a broad definition
of torture?

– Okay, I'm now going to ask you to leave. Please
leave. I'm asking you politely to leave. Please leave
this office. Now I've asked you twice politely to
leave, have you got that on record? If you don't
comply I'm going to initiate the security alert.
Right, I've called security now. They'll be here
any – (Calling) Sandra. SANDRA, get in here.
SANDRA. Where the fucking – where the –

– Okay. So, there are only a few more questions.
Is migrating to another country because you need
help actually a crime?

– Is this being filmed? Are you recording this?
Who wrote these questions for you? What's the
story here?

– The story is, I'm a twelve-year-old girl sitting
on a chair in your office asking you questions about

where you work. I am way old enough to read and comprehend books and things published on the net, and I've been reading up a lot about these things, partly because they touch my life personally but also because I am curious about them anyway, and some of the things I've read made me want to ask some questions to the people responsible, and you are one of those people.

   — Responsible for what? What are you claiming I'm responsible for? Where's the camera? Is this a news thing? Is this a paper? Is it Panorama? Are you Channel 4?

   — I guess what your story is will depend on what you do about the questions I've asked you today, and whether you do anything or nothing or something positive or something negative or something worse or something better. And I'd like to thank you very much for being so informative about how things are today.

   — Informative? How exactly have I been informative, and about what?

   — Goodbye and thank you very much, Mr Oates.

   — Hey. HEY. When was I informative? HEY.

Last night, cut a long story short, the girl said they should stay in a hotel near Edinburgh zoo.

So they did.

Brit had heard the lowing o, o, o, sound of some beast or other in a compound all night and this morning the sound of unfamiliar birds.

But get this. When she went to the desk after breakfast this morning to pay, the woman waved Brit's bank card away.

You'll be room 62 travelling with Miss Florence Smith in 68, she said.

Yes, Brit had said.

Nothing to pay, the woman said. Have a good journey.

But the look on that woman's face was one of stunnedness, the look belonging to the moment before the shock at herself doing such a thing reached her actual face.

Then they go for a train.

A ticket guy opens the gate for Florence with a bow and lets Brit through too. A ticket woman on the train asks everybody but them for tickets. When the train is delayed, the ticket woman comes into the carriage, stops at their table and apologizes for the delay as if especially to them.

You and me, kid, Brit says after the ticket woman leaves the carriage again. I'm starting to think we could conquer the world.

I'm not interested in conquering anything, Florence says.

I feel like I've run away and joined some kind of happy clappy circus, Brit says. How are you doing it?

I'm not doing anything, Florence says.

Then when they get to the station in the place on the postcard, an old guy who's lost the plot delays them even more.

Brit turns at the exit as the train's pulling out of the station and sees Florence way down at the other end of the long platform.

She sprints down the platform.

Swing your legs up, Florence is saying to a dishevelled-looking man down on the tracks.
Sit here on the side first. Then, one, two, swing them up.

Three station officials are also running towards the man, who's weeping, his arms out from his sides like he can't bear to have his own arms touch him. Two of them leap off the platform and haul him back up to platform level. Then they don't let go of him.

He lost his – what was it you lost, again? Florence is saying. Something fell on to the tracks. What was it?

My, ah, my pen, the man says.

His pen, Florence says. He dropped his pen.

It fell out of my hand, he says, I, I had it in my hand and I flicked it in the air by mistake, it flew through the air, and as it's of great sentimental, ah, uh.

A pen, a woman who's a station guard of some sort says.

Yes, the man says.

You went illegally and recklessly down on to some tracks where you could have caused a fatality or grievous hurt and trauma, the woman says. And not just to yourself but to all the people on that train that just went. Never mind us working here. Who might've suffered untold damage to our employment status too. And without regard to the effect on an already stretched timetable all up and down the country. All because you dropped a pen. Now I've heard it all. Where's this pen? I'd like to see the pen that could've lost you your life and me my job.

Here, Florence says.

She hands the man a biro Brit recognizes as one of the free pens in the hotel rooms they stayed in last night.

Brit laughs.

A Holiday Inn pen? the woman says.

Great, the man says. Sentimental.

It means a lot to him, Florence says.

The man starts crying again.

You don't have to keep hold of him like that. You can let him go now, Florence says.

The two men holding him let go of the man's arms. Then they look a little surprised at the fact that they've just done that. This makes all three station workers bluster. They kick off about how the man has committed an offence. The woman says something about police and gets out a phone.

Florence gives her a friendly look.

More a case of lost and found than offence, Florence says. Something was lost, then it got found. Didn't mean any harm. No harm done.

The woman looks at her then looks to the crying man.

However, I'm of a mind that no harm's been done in this instance, she says.

Then her face looks bewildered at hearing herself say it.

What it looks like, Brit thinks. What this feels like.

The station workers all have the same concussed look. They disappear through doors into different parts of the building and she and Florence walk the crying man to the front of the station, where the man blows his nose on his sleeve. He apologizes for doing that disgusting thing. He sits on a bench at the front of the station and he talks about how he's always liked stations because they're the places people come and go from, which means they must be places charged with emotion, and then he goes on about how once he was walking away from the station he used to come and go from in his home town, he hadn't been there for a long time but he'd come to see the stuff he'd still got in storage there after his parents had died, and when he walked away from the entrance to the station he heard someone behind him singing a bit of a song and he couldn't think what the song was, he knew it but couldn't remember its name, and the voice was a nice voice, then he remembered the song was called Every Time We Say Goodbye, and he could hear steps behind him, so he slowed down to let the person pass, and the person who passed him was a young woman, if it had been her singing she wasn't singing any more and she was way too young and wearing the wrong sort of clothes to know such an old-fashioned song or to know how to sing a song like that with such feeling.

The man stops speaking.

Good, because he is actually quite boring.

Tears start down his face again.

Brit smiles her work smile, the smile she uses when people, staff and deets both, cry on the wing.

How about we get him a coffee? she says.

212

Would you like a coffee? Florence says to the man.

He's a drunk, Brit says. There's a coffee van.

I'm not drunk. And that van doesn't do coffee, the man says.

Yes it does, Brit says. It says coffee on the side of it.

Brit goes over to the van.

When she comes back over, the man has stopped the crying thank God.

You a filmmaker? she says to him.

Of sorts, he says.

Does that mean you are or you aren't? she says.

But he gestures with his head at Florence, who's now the one crying instead.

What did you do to her? Brit says so suddenly full of protection that she has to stop herself from punching the man in the head.

He says the library's closed, Florence says.

The man takes a few steps back from the fierce look on Brit's face.

Well, it is, the man says. It's true. It's closed on a Tuesday.

That's no problem, Brit says.

She puts an arm round Florence.

That's nothing to cry about, she says. We can go to another library. We can go to one in a bigger town.

I really needed the library here to be open, Florence says.

We can easy look up whatever you need on my phone, Brit says. Library in my pocket. Here. What do you need to look up?

I've got to get to the place on the card, Florence says, then get to the library in the place. I don't have any other message, or any more message, than that.

Brit takes her by the shoulders and turns her towards the coffee van.

See that woman over there, in there? she says.

Florence wipes an eye and looks.

Do you know her?

Florence shakes her head.

Well, she knows you, Brit says.

How? Florence says.

She just asked me straight out whether you're Florence, Brit says.

Who is she? Florence says.

Funny, that's pretty much the question she just asked me, Brit says. I went over there to buy some coffee and she said she didn't do coffee.

And then she said, is that girl standing over there next to the man you're with by any chance named Florence?

And I didn't say anything. And then she looked me up and down and she said,

I've already made the acquaintance of Mr Filmmaker but who might you be when you're at home, Mrs SA4A Uniform?

So I said,

thing is, Mrs Coffee Van That Isn't A Fucking Coffee Van. I'm not at home right now. I'm a long, long way from home. And that means I might be anybody. Anybody at all.

March. It can be pretty hard going.

Lion and lamb. The cold shoulder of spring.

Month of the kind of blossom that could still be snow, month of the papery unsheathing of the heads of the daffodils. The soldiers' month, it takes its name from Mars, the Roman war god; in Gaelic it's the winter-spring, and in Old Saxon the rough month, because of the roughness of its winds.

But it's also the lengthening-month, the one when the day begins to stretch. Month of madnesses and unexpected mellownesses, month of new life. Before the Gregorian calendar the new year started not in January but in March, to celebrate both the vernal equinox with its tilt of the North towards the sun again, and the Feast of the Annunciation, the day the angel appears to the Virgin Mary and announces that even though she's a virgin she'll conceive, and by good Spirit.

Surprise. Happy new year. Everything impossible is possible.

The air lifts. It's the scent of commencement, initiation, threshold. The air lets you know quite ceremonially that something has changed. Primroses deep in the ivy throw wide the arms of their leaves. Colour slashes across the everyday. The deep blue of grape hyacinths, the bright yellows in wastelands catching the eyes of the people on trains. Birds visit the leafless trees, but not leafless like in winter; now the branches stiffen, the ends of the twigs glow like low-burning candles.

Then the rain, and the first sign of the branch splitting open to blossom on the old tree, the light inside visible in the wood, you can see it even at night under the streetlamp.

If you rise at dawn in a clear sky, and during the month of March, they say you can catch a bag of air so intoxicated with the essence of spring that when it is distilled and prepared, it will produce an oil of gold, remedy enough to heal all ailments.

That's the voice of the artist Tacita Dean, who in the mid 1990s, when she was thirty years old and the artist in residence for a year at L'École Nationale des Beaux Arts de Bourges in France, decided it was time to try to do something she'd always wanted to do when she was a child – to catch and keep a cloud, maybe even start a cloud collection.

She made a plan to go up in a hot air balloon and catch some cloud in a bag.

But of course it's impossible to catch, keep or own a cloud.

Also, hot air balloons, as she discovered, can only fly in the spring if the sky is cloudless.

So she decided she'd go up in the balloon and catch mist instead.

To be sure to find some mist she went further south, to mountainous country, Lans en Vercors near Grenoble, where the morning sky was bound to be misty.

The balloon rose. The sky cleared. The day became one of the clearest days for that time of the year in the place's living memory. Floating above the mountains covered in snow, what she bagged was pure clear air.

As it happens, the day she chose to catch this air was exactly the time of year that alchemists say is the best time to collect dew *on its voyage from Earth to Heaven*. Ancient alchemy says you need dew that's been gathered over a thousand days to distil and manufacture the kind of elixir that can make all sorts of things better.

Dean made a short film, less than three minutes long, of her journey to catch the air. It's called A Bag of Air.

Up goes the huge hot air balloon. Its shadow gets smaller on the ground and in the film frame the higher it gets. Out come the hands of the artist. Into the clear plastic bag goes some air, then the bag in her hands is twisted and knotted, like a small balloon itself. Then she does the same thing again, a new bag, different air, caught and knotted, the same.

The film is a piece of pure joke-vision. But in it, breathing takes flight. Alchemy and transformation become matters of good spirit. Something dismissible and ridiculous – and magic if you'll let it be – happens in front of your eyes.

Then the three minutes of black and white film are over and what's left is the story of human beings and air, something we hardly ever notice or think about, something we can't live without.

3

Now for 140 seconds of cutting edge realism:

SHUT UP just shut the fUck Up can someone tape her mouth shut she deserve to be relentlesly abused what a Cunt go and die hang yourself you ugly Cunt we are all having a laugh at you You are a shit show nobody couldn't play fuck marry kill with you its just Kill you are a Tampon you are odios you deseve to be raped left for dead your Daughter deserves to be raped and stabed to death with a Kitchen KNnife your like a broken record bleeding heart liberal fuck WE know where you Live we now where your kid goes to school shut Up if you don't shut YOU mouth we will shut it for you you will be shut up WTF You think you doing you bring these Attacks on yourself fucking disgusting fucking fucking yuo disgust me you need raped you need anil raped you will be anil raped then rape in

223

your cakehole then dead kill yourself hang yours elf
you fat Arse ugly cunt you need to be poked with a
massive Dildo you are typical muslim black faGGot
you are simplY unforgivable beyond the pail people
like You are destroying the Western World so full of
shit jimmy savile should have raped you in Hospital
you are disabled because God Hates You nex time
you are out on a dark night we will get you good
and you children you should be scared you imigrant
shit you need hate maile to Sort you out you deserve
hate you Scrotum face arseole face you are a pedo
for fkc sake I cant stand you you are a fukcing Joke
you should be force to feed and house a bunch of
violence foreign invaders see how you like it fat
retard bitch slag slut TRAITOR TRAITER
hypocrite your children will Die you are a failure in
Life everybody can see you worthless piece of shit
go and drink some floor polish drink some
disnfectant you flithy queer immgrant suck my
DICK pig ugly jog on

It was the time of the year when everything was dead. I mean dead in a way that meant it seemed that nothing would ever live again.

The sky was a massive closed door. The cloud was dull metal. The trees were bare and broken. The ground was ungiving. The grass was dead. The birds were absent. The fields were frozen ruts of earth and the deadness went down under the surface for miles.

Everywhere the people were afraid. Food stocks were low. The barns were almost empty.

This was the time of the year, traditionally, at which the sages, the elders, the youths, the maidens, the very old people and the people wearing masks and bearskins so they could masquerade as ancient ancestors risen from the dust, all decided that the only way to make life come back to the world was to choose a young woman from among the maidens and sacrifice her as a gift to the gods by making her dance herself to death.

The gods, according to tradition, like a death. They like a pure death. So the purer the maiden the better. And she was usually a really good dancer, the one they chose, especially chosen so she'd be a particularly spectacular high-kicking sacrifice.

The day came. The whole of the village gathered. The sage had painted himself bright silver with hope. Everyone turned up to watch, even the 300-year-old woman, poking around with her walking stick in the fallow furrows. Everyone raised their fists in the air and did a bit of a dance to get things going.

Then the dance of the maidens began.

It was mesmerizing. It went like clockwork. It turned all the maidens into a single piece of choreographed machinery, made them into nothing but its components. It circled and jerked, jerked and circled.

At last the circle opened to reveal the chosen girl, a young and brilliant maiden with her whole life ahead of her. The dance opened to her at the same time as it closed on her.

What was supposed to happen now was that she was meant to fall to the earth. Then she was to start pawing at the ground like a beast, then to do a wild dance until she flailed herself to death.

Then everyone would celebrate, because everything would start to grow again.

But what happened was this.

The girl at the centre of things folded her arms. She shook her head. She stood and tapped her foot.

I'm not a symbol, she said.

The dance stopped.

The music stopped.

The villagers gasped out loud.

She said it louder.

I'm not your symbol. Go and lose yourself or find yourself in some other story. Whatever you're looking for, you're not going to find it by making me or anyone like me do some dance for you.

The villagers stood on the world stage not knowing what to do. Some of them looked aghast. Some of them looked bored. Some of the maidens began a fluttery panic because if not this girl it'd be one of them who'd have to dance to death.

It's unnecessary, the girl said. Come on. We can all think of a better way to do this.

Some of the villagers grew angry; others looked at the scenery, looked askance. A couple of them looked pleased. An ancestor took his bear-mask off and wiped sweat off his forehead; it's hard to wear those costumes for any length of time.

There are much less bloody ways to hope for spring, the girl said. Better ways of working fruitfully with the climate and the seasons, than by sacrificing people to them. And anyway, you're only doing it because some of you get off on the brutality. One or two people always do, always will. And the rest of you are worried that if you don't do what everybody else is doing then the ones who get off on it might decide to choose you for the next sacrifice.

Some of the audience, out beyond the villagers in the rows of seats in the theatre, were also getting pretty angry. They'd come to see a classic. They weren't getting what they'd paid for. Critics were shaking their heads. Critics wrote furiously on their screens with their little iPad pens. They tapped furiously at their iPhones.

People like a good riot.

The gods, however, laughed.

One of them nodded to the others, reached down, scooped the girl into invisible god-sized hands and transformed her into herself. The god did this in the blink of an eye so fast that no villagers, no audience, even noticed it happen. But the gods had given that girl an armour that sealed itself round her. The girl felt real strength go through her like a god-breath.

Real strength was a matter of sensing something alive in you bigger than just your own breathing.

Then the 300-year-old woman stepped forward. She'd know how to deal with this.

Tell us a bit about yourself, dearie, she said in her ancient voice.

But the girl just laughed.

As you well know, old lady, that'd be the first step towards me vanishing altogether, she said. Because as soon as you all hear me say anything about myself, I'll stop meaning me. I'll start meaning you.

A murmur went through the crowd.

My mother told me, *they'll want you to tell them your story*, the girl said. My mother said, *don't. You are not anyone's story.*

The 300-year-old woman made a gigantic effort to pull herself a little more upright. She flared a nostril like she could smell something unpleasant.

What if we sacrifice you anyway? she said. Regardless of how willing or unwilling you are?

The girl laughed carefree.

You can try, she said. Kill me anyway. No doubt you will. But you know as well as I do, though I'm so young and you're so old, that I'm older and wiser right now than you've ever been.

A gasp went through everyone onstage, and everyone offstage, and all the millions of viewers on the web.

The girl laughed even louder.

Go on, the girl said. Do your worst. See if it makes things better.

12.33 on the coffee truck dashboard clock – but who cares what time it is? Richard is free of time, maybe for the first time ever. He is giddy with wide-open afterlife, travelling through a 30mph zone at 60mph (he can see the speedo, he's practically sitting in the driver's seat) with a woman on either side of him, now that's the way to do it. He is getting a lift to the nearest city. The woman called Alda is taking these people somewhere and asked him if he wanted a lift too and he said yes and now they're all in the front because there's nowhere to sit in the back except on the linoleum down between the cupboards and the machines. The girl who gave him the pen is jammed against the passenger door. He himself is sardined between the women, one of his legs on each side of the stick. It is lucky the truck is an automatic or it'd have been a bit tricky.

The seats are very nice, done in bright brown leather. These trucks are snazzy on the inside. The doors on the driver's cabin open with a nod to the retro, like continental doors, the opposite way from doors on normal cars or trucks. But the steering wheel's on the right, like it should be. It's gimmicky, but impressive all the same.

What's that place over there? he says. On the hill. The castle.

That's not a castle, the coffee truck woman says. It's Ruthven Barracks.

The coffee truck woman's name is Alda Lyons. She told them outside the station. She's one of the town's librarians.

Where the Jacobite rebellion ended, she says. Burned down the day after Culloden.

Day after what? Richard says.

Culloden, she says.

Thought that's what you said, Richard says. Culloden. A very good film.

It's not just a film, Alda says. It's a battle. And a place.

Yes, Richard says. Film too. A very good one, Peter Watkins. Last battle of the English against the Scots.

Well, she says (very like a librarian). Hanoverians against the Jacobites. But folk do like to simplify. Things do simplify over time. Ruthven Barracks was burned down in April 1746. What was left of the Jacobite army gathered at the barracks on the day after the battle, they were waiting to see what to do next, and the message came through from Bonnie Prince Charlie saying the fight was over and every man was to fend for himself. So they set fire to it so the other army couldn't use it any more, and went on their way.

Watkins made the film about the nuclear strike that they were too scared to show, Richard says. War Game.

I remember, Alda says. I remember his Culloden too.

Culloden, Richard says. Culloden.

So good they named it twice, Alda says.

I'm repeating the way you say it, Richard says, because I've been saying it wrong all my life. I've been saying *Cull*oden.

Even though you saw that film and the film was so good, Alda says. Eh?

Cassandra here, next to me, the young woman in the security guard uniform says. She knows a fact or two about nuclear strikes that she was terrifying me with yesterday.

Eternal nuclear autumn, the schoolgirl says. We are now globally just five nuclear explosions away from it becoming the only season that we'll have on this planet.

Five. Is that all? Alda says.

Possibly less, the girl says. Given that I am twelve

years old, and there are just twelve years left to stop the world being ruined by climate change, I'd say there's an urgency the age of me to do something to stop it.

Thought your name was Florence, the man says.

I am capable of being a person of more than one name, the girl says.

Me too, Alda says.

I meant Cassandra like the prophet in legend, the security guard says, who told people what was true about the future but nobody ever believed a word she said.

The security guard is the girl's friend or family. Her name is Britt, like Ekland he supposes. (Though she is actually nothing like Britt Ekland, more's the pity.

Sexist. Man with no emotional intelligence.

Very true. But maybe a little harsh on yourself, his imaginary daughter says.)

That Ruthven location, Richard says. Is it beautiful? I'm looking for a place.

For making a film? the girl says.

No, he says. For a friend of mine who died recently. I'm looking for a place where I can just send, you know. A thought, a nod of the head, into the sky in a beautiful place for her. Which is why, I think, I came north in the first place.

I can think of much better places to do something like that, Alda says.

When did your friend die? the girl asks.

August, he says.

That's not very long ago, Alda says. I'm sorry.

Thank you, he says. She was a scriptwriter, often my scriptwriter. I was lucky to work with her. The best. You're far too young to have seen some of what she did, in fact you maybe all are. 1960s, 70s, 80s, if you watched TV in those decades you'll have seen something by her, you'll be bound to have, you'll never have forgotten it if you did, and even if you have, it'll be somewhere inside you. A very great talent, very undersung.

Alda jerks a thumb back in the direction of the ruin they passed.

It's beautiful there, sure, she says. But the history. Not so beautiful.

Ah, he says. Right.

The systematic controlling of peoples by other peoples, Alda says. The fight, the destruction, the defeat.

Was your friend a defeated person? the girl says.

It's just not a word I can associate with her in any way, he says.

Well, not there then, Alda says. They built the barracks on top of a castle or two that'd already been burned down. It's been like it is now since 1746, probably because if they'd built on top of it someone else would've burned down whatever they built. The new British government first built the

235

barracks after the Act of Union, they wanted to make more money out of their new land. So they militarized it. It was a military zone for about a century here. Especially after Culloden. Then sporting estates. Deerpark.

Far too mountainous for people to ever live here, Richard says. But then that's what's beautiful about the Highlands. It's so beautifully deserted everywhere.

He watches a flush going up the neck of Alda the coffee truck woman; it spreads up to her ear from under the collar of her jacket.

No, this was a thriving busy place, she says. Quite definitely populated, much busier than it is now. Not that the Clearances made an impact here anything like how badly they did elsewhere in the north.

The clearance, Richard says.

Clearan*ces*, Alda says. Another new word for your collection.

As in sales, in shops that are closing? the girl says.

As in when the English ruling class, with the help of the corrupt clan chief landowners, systematically cut down the population of the Highlands, Alda says, and this is only 200 years ago, a blink of history's eye, and by systematically cut down I mean they treated people much like you'd cut down brushwood or gorse, and then wrote in the papers that they were improving the area, *pacifying its wild savages*. They were clever, the people who'd lived here. They had to be. It's very tough farming terrain, but they'd worked it out and made it work, for them, against the odds, for centuries. Those wild unbridled savages I'm descended from.

Filmmaker, yeah? like a film director? the security guard Britt says.

He tilts his head towards her and says it with irony.

Yes, like a film director.

Yeah? she says. Really?

TV mainly, he says. For my sins. I'm from a time when anything progressive on TV was quite often thought to be a kind of sin.

She starts to tell him a long story about a film she saw on TV once that she's never forgotten. But Richard stops listening because the radio, on at low volume in the truck, is playing the old pop song about joy and fun in seasons in the sun by the man with the thin sounding voice, singing about how he's going to die soon and how he's saying goodbye to all his friends, and Richard has just remembered this:

one night in 1970-something, 3? 4?, Paddy phoning, waking him up.

Doubledick, I need you here right now. If you can, can you?

2.45am. He flags down a taxi in the rain.

A pre-adolescent twin opens the front door.

You mother called me, he says. What's wrong?

Coming through the wall is music, quite loud for 3am.

You're here, Paddy says. Good. We don't know what to do. It's worst in my bedroom but the boys can hear it in theirs too right through at the back of the house. The bathroom's the only place there's any respite. But we can't all sleep in the bath.

The song finishes; the music stops.

There we go, Richard says.

Paddy raises her eyebrows.

The song starts up again.

Ah, Richard says.

Paddy and the twin laugh. The other twin, in a bedroom somewhere behind them, laughs too.

What is it? Richard says.

Number one in the charts right now, one twin says.

Terry Jacks. Seasons in the Sun, the other calls through.

You've tried phoning them, Richard says.

Dial-a-disc, the twin on the landing says.

Both twins crack up laughing.

We've phoned, Paddy says, we've rung a doorbell, we've knocked at the back and the front and hammered on their walls. We've thrown stones at their windows. You might say we're pretty damn certain they're not in.

It's been playing since half past four this afternoon, the twin in the bedroom calls.

The stylus'll wear out, Richard says.

Diamond. Could be days, the first twin says.

Police? Richard says.

Paddy gives him a withering look.

She won't call the police and she won't let us call the police, the twin in the bedroom shouts through.

What if someone's dead in there? he says.

Even if they were she still wouldn't let us call the police, the other twin says.

If they're in there and not already dead I'll happily oblige, the bedroom twin shouts.

The song finishes and starts again.

And even if the Hardwicks *are* dead in there, the other twin says, Terry Jacks is proving immortal.

More than forty years later, Richard remembers how he'd climbed on to a flat roof and jemmied a window, hoisted himself into an empty house, followed the tune through to the lounge and lifted the arm on a record player, how he'd taken the single off the turntable and brought it back to Paddy's, and how then at four in the morning she put a pencil through its turntable hole and all four of them sat and watched, drank coffee, that instant kind everybody drank with powdered milk, while a twin held the 45 as close as he could to the gas fire with all its elements lit.

Then Richard went back in through the window

he'd left open and put the single, folded in half, on the carpet next to their record player with a note under it saying One Too Many Seasons In The Sun.

He closed and snibbed the window to make it seem like no one had been in, and he left by the back door, which he unlocked with a key he found on the upper ledge of the doorframe. He locked it again with this key. He gave the key to Paddy.

In case Terry Jacks ever rises from the dead, he said.

That made both twins laugh.

He laughs now – on a road in another country on a journey with a bunch of people he's never met.

It's like the 60s all over again.

He is not dead.

Ha ha!

He smiles at the woman in the security uniform in delight. She gives him a really strange look.

The amazing thing about remembering this story, after all the years, is that he is actually feeling affection for the twins. Sweet Dermot laughing. Sweet soft-hearted little Patrick with his hands over his face laughing.

The woman in the uniform is clearly waiting for him to say something back to her. The girl is looking to him expectantly too. But he has no idea what anyone's been saying.

Sometimes, he says, we don't know why people do what they do. But we can only do our best, the best we can do, in response, and try to be as good-humoured as possible while we do it.

I don't see that there was much chance for him to be good-humoured about it, the security guard says. Since the Nazis were obviously about to shoot him in the head.

The Nazis?

Uh.

Richard tries to think of something suitable to say.

An awful time, he says. Truly. I always feel so relieved not to have had to live through it. Always on television now, always the same awful pieces of footage, the same faces, same thugs shouting don't buy from Jews, same shopfronts with the slogans painted on them, same terrorized bullied people being filmed walking towards trains or away from them in the mud, same old Hitler shouting footage. As if such terrible history's a kind of entertainment. All that poison. All that anger. All that brutality. All that loss. You'd think we'd learn from it. But no, instead we play it on repeat, let it play away in the corner of the room while we go on with our lives regardless. Terrible times, easily resurrected. Type in some words, up it comes on any screen. It's a bit like that song playing a minute ago on the radio. I have this same thought in supermarkets too when they play, you know, music from decades ago as if it's the soundtrack of now. Well, it *is* the soundtrack

241

of now. It's as if. As if someone hobbled a horse. Made it hard for it to move forward without something dragging it back.

The security woman thanks him.

Pleasure, he says.

He winks over at the girl who got him off the rails. There are so many people in this front cabin of the truck that she is pressed hard against the door and can hardly turn her head.

You all right there? he says.

I'm okay, she says. I'm doing my best in response to my situation and being as good-humoured as I can while I'm doing it.

Everybody laughs.

Anyone driving towards them and past them at that moment will have seen an image Richard knows he'd have liked to have caught on film.

Think you're funny, the security guard says.

I *am* funny, the girl says.

Funny in the head, the security guard says.

Then there's a silence in the truck except for the song called The Final Countdown on the radio, which Alda reaches over and switches off.

Better? she says to Richard.

I'm sorry, he says. Didn't mean to complain.

But look, she says. You were right. That's us completely unhobbled now.

She puts her foot down. The truck speeds up.

They can go at quite a lick, these trucks.

242

How far is it? the girl asks again.

The battlefield, Alda says. Well now.

We're going to a battlefield? Richard says. *The* battlefield?

How far? the girl asks.

Tell her how far, the security guard says.

Not far, Alda says.

In units of minute, hour, day, week or month? the girl says.

It's, by my estimate, let's see now, Alda says. One legend and a couple of old songs away.

Songs? Britt says. Is she going to sing?

Did you know, Alda says, that the word slogan was a Gaelic word originally? Your man there saying the word reminded me. From the words for the shout of the army. Sluagh-ghairm. Slogan. It means war cry. Tells you all you need to know about what slogans are always about, whether it's take back control or leave means leave or don't buy from Jews or I'm lovin' it or just do it or every little helps.

He's not my man, the security guard says.

I don't care what language the time passes in, the girl says. So long as it passes.

April 1st, 1976: a day as full of all the usual possibilities as any old day; day of deeply troubling news stories, day of *narrative strategy and reality,* day of the word *symbiotic,* whatever it might mean, above all, day of an unexpected very good fuck, one towards which, Richard finally understands, he has always been travelling hopefully, since that's what love is, this matter of hopeful travel against the usual deeply troubling odds.

Why do you call me Doubledick? he says afterwards with his head on her arm in her bed.

Why what, darling man? Paddy says.

(Paddy, right next to him, is what she calls away with the fairies.)

It's in honour of my exceptional prowess, isn't it? he says.

What is? she says. Oh. Doubledick. Ha.

Obviously I'd like to think it is, he says. But since you've been calling me it for years, ever since we first met, I know it can't be anything to do with an exceptional prowess you've only experienced for the first time today. Unless you've been imagining me. Which means that right now, God forbid, you may well be a bit disappointed.

She laughs.

Nothing to do with your dick, Dick, she says.

Oh. Oh well, he says.

And I like a good fuck as much as the next person, and that was a very good fuck. Thanks. No, your double name's lifted from an old Charles Dickens story.

Oh, he says. Now *I'm* a bit disappointed.

Not a very famous story, she says, but one about a young man who's got the same name as you.

Richard or Lease? Richard says.

Story of Richard Doubledick, Paddy says. When we first met, and you told me your name was Richard, I'd never met a Richard other than this fictional one, so the word that followed your name in my head, quite naturally did and always will, is Doubledick. And now you've taken on the shape of the words.

As the scriptwriter said to the naked man, Richard says. How does it go?

Quite a bit of the old up and down in the plot, Paddy says. So you've got this young man, his name's Richard Doubledick, and he's enlisted as a soldier. He's not a great soldier – he's not a great anything. He's had a bad start in life, a terrible childhood, he's an unhappy soul, very lost in life, so miserable with himself that he's taken to troublemaking. But then an officer takes an interest in him, befriends him, helps him sort himself out, treats him like family. Very soon Doubledick becomes a first-class fighting machine. Then that officer is killed in battle and Richard Doubledick is heartbroken. He declares he'll avenge the death if it's the last thing he does and that he'll spend his whole life devoted to that vengeance.

So. The years pass –

They do, Richard says. They will.

– and he falls in love, Paddy says, and gets married to a lovely woman, someone he loves with his whole heart. He goes to meet her people, and he realizes when he arrives at their family seat for the first time that he's married into the heart of the family of the very officer who killed his beloved captain.

Ah, Richard says.

I know, she says.

Well, what does he do?

Isn't that the question, Paddy says. Isn't that always the question. Because what he does is why this story is a great story. He lets go of the bitterness. He decides to let bygones be bygones. And the story ends prophetically, in a vision of the son of one side of the family fighting alongside the son of the other side of the family on the same side against a common enemy, French and English in the same trench together. War won't stop, the story says. But enmity can. Things can change over time, what looks fixed and pinned and closed in a life can change and open, and what's unthinkable and impossible at one time will be easily possible in another.

I was a girl when I read it, just turned thirteen. It was my very last schoolday. My life right then had no possibles. My father was newly dead, there was no money, we had to go out to work, even my littlest sister, she was eleven. We weren't stupid, none of us was. My father, a brilliant man, wasted. Found dead on a road he'd helped make. I mean a road he'd been a labourer on. We'd no chance. And the police were brutal fuckers. It was a brutal time. One of our older sisters, too, dead that year. Maggie. Tuberculosis. Nineteen years old, funny and nimble she was, I can see her now in my head turning on her heel and making light of something, she loved the dancing, loved kissing a boy or two, and we were very alike, her and me. The town photographer had taken our photo, remember how they still colourized photos by hand then, and he'd chosen me out of the whole family and coloured my cheeks the same red as he did hers. Which only added to my feeling I'd next to no chance.

So I'm in the library and there's an empty fire grate in the library, the nuns weren't much on warmth, I'm sitting next to it out of a hope that an empty grate might still hold a bit of heat. I sit with the book in my hands and I think to myself, this is maybe the last day I'll ever have the chance to sit and hold a book.

We'd no books of our own. We didn't have books.

I'd picked the first that came to hand off the shelf. I was determined, I was going to read a story from its start to its finish if it was the last thing I did. And I thought as I turned its pages, my life is as empty a hearth as that one, I'm the ashes in that grate.

But time's factory's a secret place, that's Charles Dickens again. Sometimes we're lucky. With a bit of help and a bit of luck, we get to be more than the one thing or the nothing that history'd have us be. We're only here by the grace and the work of others. I am anyway. *Here's to those others who helped*, that's my prayer when I go to my bed, *and may I be such an other to a good many myself.*

I'm definitely here right now by the grace of you, Richard says.

I don't think that place you've your hand on is generally called grace, Paddy says. But come on then, will we make it a double, Dick?

That's what I call living up to my reputation, he says.

Afterwards they make up jokes about Hard Times and she invents funny imaginary sex acts that might be given the name Doubledickens. Then Paddy sends him downstairs to make a pot of tea and when he comes back up with the tea things on a tray she's showered, got all her clothes back on again and they drink the tea.

And that's that.

He opens one eye for a moment to check on the time. 13.04 on the clock next to the speedo. The woman called Alda is singing a song in a language that sounds like it would if your subconscious had a language and could sing.

He closes the eye.

The child Paddy at age thirteen is sitting by an empty grate holding a book in her folded arms pressed to her chest like a talisman.

She is so thin he can see right through her.

Behind her there's a line of children that goes so far back it never stops. They're in clothes as ragged as suits of dead leaves. Their hands are the only things small enough to reach inside the industrial machines and clean out the oily gunk and the fibres, of which their lungs are already full. But no hand can go inside and clean out their lungs.

Thank God those days are over, he thinks.

Thank God it's better in the world right now.

Update yourself, the child Paddy says.

She sounds very like his imaginary daughter.

Kids down the mines right now, she says, right this minute, right this very 13.04. You know there are. They're mining the cobalt for all the environmentally sound electric cars.

Kids right now in the rags of Hello Kitty clothes sitting in slave labour sheds hitting old dead batteries with hammers to get metals out of them that poison them as soon as they touch them.

Kids eating rubbish on landfill mountains.

Kids of all ages who're good for sex money, used and filmed and swapped and filmed again, the money changing hands up over their heads right now, 13.04. Thousands of kids who don't know where their parents are, whether they're alive or dead, whether they'll ever see parents again, kids locked in freezing cold warehouses in the US. Right now. In these days you've just called *better in the world*. Kids by themselves all over this country, who get here by crossing the world then just disappear. Not forgetting the hundreds of thousands of kids born and living here, surviving on God knows what, on air, in a whole new version of the same old British poverty.

A thousand thousand thousand of us. And if they, I mean we, don't sew fast enough, the line of children stretching away for miles behind the child Paddy tells him, then the people running the factory hold our hands under the needles, make us put our feet on the footpumps and press down and sew

251

thread through our own hands. There isn't a T-shirt in existence, there isn't a common chocolate bar we haven't a hand in the making of. There isn't a history we're not deep in the pigfat of the money of. We're the factory. We're eaten alive. That makes us the hungriest ghosts. And you're poor thin things for us to survive off, that's a fact.

It's definitely Paddy, the voice speaking.

So has his imaginary daughter maybe been the child Paddy all along?

When he thinks this, the ragged child in his head spits fire at him. Her hand is on fire. She waves it at him to get his attention. Embers drip off her fingers, fall and smash open on the ground at her feet in little burning fractures of light.

Stop making it all about you, Doubledick, she says. Wake yourself up, for Christ sake.

13.05 when he opens his eyes.

He opens them because the haunting singing has stopped.

They're driving over the brow of a hill and the view has opened very prettily below them to a body of water, a bridge, a glinting city.

Where are we? he says.

Where were *you*? Alda says.

Your songs came over me like lullaby, he says. Like the unconscious has a language it can speak in. The unconscious, the subconscious, I've never known the difference. What I mean is, it sounded like one of them was singing.

I know you mean well, but it's a conscious and everyday and very real language, Alda says. But thanks for your, eh. What'll we call it? Romanticism, I suppose.

Sedative songs, the security woman says. You could market them on the net. Make a fortune.

Thanks, Alda says. I think.

Where we are is nearly there, yes? the girl says.

An urgent child, Richard says. Best impetus in the world.

I just have to stop off in town for a couple of things, Alda says. We weren't expecting to be picking up quite so many of you today.

She turns to Richard.

And when you said that thing about your friend dying, she says. Something I wanted to ask you. I was wondering if you might maybe have had something to do with the TV play from years ago, it was called Andy Hoffnung. Did you?

Richard rubs his forehead, puts the heel of his hand in one eye.

Am I dreaming? he asks the girl.

You're awake enough to have offended Alda about the Gaelic language and to have offended me by referring to me as a child, the girl says.

Then I'm definitely here, he says. But I may still be asleep. Being perfectly capable of causing offence in my sleep too.

He turns to Alda.

I made Andy Hoffnung, he says.

You're the director Richard Lease, she says.

I am, he says.

!

He is so amazed at what she's saying that he
forgets to back it up with the usual for my sins.

Sea of Troubles, she says.

Yes! he says.

The Panharmonicon, she says.

The Panharmonicon, he says. Good God.

My favourite when I was a kid, Alda says. Well,
teenage.

Nobody remembers The Panharmonicon these
days, Richard says. I'd even forgotten The
Panharmonicon myself.

I loved it so much, she says. The writer's your
friend that just died, is that right? The one you were
talking about. I saw in the paper.

She did, he says. My friend.

I'm sorry, she says. I read the thing in the paper
and I thought, that's the woman who wrote all
those plays. Patricia Heal.

That's her, he says. Actually, the idea for The
Panharmonicon came out of work she was doing
on Andy Hoffnung, she'd spent a lot of time in the
library reading up about Beethoven for Hoffnung
and listening to the music, and she'd come across,
you know, the story of the man asking Beethoven
to write the piece of music for his orchestra
machine.

Panharmonicon, the girl says. Like in the Magic
Kaladesh card deck?

Richard blinks.

Beethoven was a composer in the eighteenth and nineteenth century, he says, and –

Uh huh, I know who *Beethoven* is, the girl says. I'm asking about the music box. There's a picture of something with the same name in my little brother's card deck. But go on. Beethoven was a composer in the eighteenth and nineteenth centuries, and?

I'm definitely not dreaming if I'm managing to offend over such a broad scale of topics, Richard says.

He tells them what he can remember about The Panharmonicon.

Beethoven had a friend, the man who invented the metronome, who made a machine that could mimic a complete orchestra. This friend asked Beethoven to write him a piece of music he could demonstrate his machine to the public with. So Beethoven did.

It was about quarter of an hour long, Richard tells them, it was called Wellington's Victory, and it enacted a battle between French and English tunes. Massively popular piece at the time. Nobody much remembers it now. It sets Rule Britannia and the national anthem against the tune of For He's a Jolly Good Fellow, which is originally a French tune, not English at all, and is a song about a famous duke who goes off to war and gets himself killed, and a tree grows out of his grave, and a bird sits in the tree. And so on.

Richard tells them how Beethoven wrote it so that the inventor could demonstrate not just the sounds the machine could make but also an early stereo effect.

So the music takes sides, he says. Quite literally. Some of it happens on one side of your hearing and some of it happens on the other. It's how you know which side's won. The drums aping the cannons die out on one side sooner than on the other.

And Paddy, everybody called her Paddy, my friend, and she called herself Paddy. Well, Paddy loved this. And she took the germ of it and wrote the script about an argument between the two sides of the road in an English village, about which side thinks it has the most right to the grass verge in the middle where they park their cars, and what happens when one side of the road takes what it calls control.

Carnage, Alda says. Car carnage. It's brilliant. The burning ice-cream van. They should reshow it, right now. It couldn't be more timeless, or more timely. It's like she could see the future.

She was brilliant, Richard says. Is brilliant.

I loved the boy character, Alda says.

That actor went on to have roles in all sorts of films, Richard says. Go-Between, Equus, Midnight Express. Then he went to Hollywood, I don't know what happened to him after that.

He was wonderful, Alda says.

Dennis, Richard says.

Dennis, yes, Alda says. With his cello. Scared to take it to school any more because of the thuggy kids who hassle him.

And he goes and sits on the top of the town hill with the girl from the other side of the road who he likes and who likes him, Eleonora, her family's Italian, with the ice-cream van the neighbours set fire to. And they watch the smoke rise from the burning cars, Richard says, and they talk very seriously about why they both think their own side's got the right to the piece of grass. They nearly fight. And then Leo, he calls her Leo, starts laughing, she says look how stupid what's happening down there looks from up here. And then so does he, he starts laughing. And then the end – them standing together at one end of the road they live on, watching the neighbours on both sides throwing rocks at the houses opposite. And she starts to sing a tune, and he plays a different tune, and then the two tunes match up and become one tune.

And how for a moment, Alda says, for an unbelievable moment, when the tunes meet and sound so fine together, the people stop throwing their stones and all turn and stare at them and listen.

And a split second after, they're back at it throwing the rocks at each other's houses again, Richard says. And then their parents come out of the crowd and drag them off to the different sides of the road they live on.

The cello lying there on the concrete with the burnt-out cars and bits of brick round it, Alda says.

A very vivid ending, Richard says.

That's not the ending, Alda says.

Yes it is, Richard says.

The ending is them by themselves in the train carriage, Alda says. Leaving the village. Off out into the world. With each other.

Oh, Richard says. Oh. You're quite right. So it is. So it was.

Those old train carriage compartments with six seats, Alda says. The door's closed, you can't hear what they're saying through the glass, it's private to them now, they look out to check nobody's on to them or following them, then the train shunts forward and they fall into each other, start doing a funny dance together, then we see the outside of the train and then the village from above, and the train leaving it, and then up and up, so you see how it all looks, how small, from a flying bird's view.

Richard smiles.

The God shot, he says. Cost more than the rest of it put together, I had to sweat blood to get it. Can't believe I forgot that. You know it better than I do. And I made it.

What happened to the girl who played Leo? Alda says.

Tracy something, he says. Carry On Emmannuelle, Persil advert. After that, I don't know.

The richness of our culture, Alda says.

The security woman starts singing a song to the tune of For He's a Jolly Good Fellow.

The bear went over the mountain, she sings. The bear went over the mountain. The bear went over the mountain. But it was a waste of time. Cause all there was was more mountain, and all there was was more mountain. All there was was more mountain. So the bear just stayed at home.

Everybody in the coffee truck joins in, guessing the words as they go along.

The truck pulls into the car park of a big supermarket.

Are we here? the girl says. Is this it?

No, Alda says.

Not to be acting too like a, you know. Child. But are we nearly, and how far now, and how much longer, and other questions of that sort, the girl says.

Tell her how far and how long, the security woman says to Alda.

As long as a piece of string and about as far as I intend to throw you both, Alda says to the woman.

She opens her door. She comes round and opens the passenger door and catches the girl as she falls out.

They all stand in the car park round the coffee truck.

That's you in Inverness, then, Mr Lease, Alda says. There's buses from over there down into town if you don't want to walk down. I'm sorry not to be able to take you further. I can't believe I got to meet the man who made those Play for Todays. Made my day.

My year, he says. My decade.

What are the chances of that, eh? she says.

She hugs him shyly. He hugs her shyly back.

He says goodbye to the security woman.

Bye then, she says.

He glances over at the girl.

I believe I owe you, he says.

Actually, she says, if we subscribe to the traditions, you'll find I'm now officially responsible for you for the rest of your life. But I'm not so bothered about some of the traditions, so you're lucky.

Lucky to meet you, he says.

He takes the Holiday Inn pen out of his pocket.

I'll let you off your responsibilities in return for you letting me keep this, he says.

But she's already off, turned towards her future.

They head for the supermarket, leaving him behind. He stands by himself in a car park in a city strange to him, thrown back into the story of his life.

1.33 on the clock above the main entrance of the supermarket.

A man is looking hard at some lemons.

The skin of a lemon is pitted, like skin slightly goosebumped or roughened.

The snub end of a lemon is reminiscent of the nipple on a breast like the breasts on the statues of the perfect beauties in the Rome museums, the breast on the statue of the woman whose hands are turning into twigs in the Villa Borghese.

Picture of a changed woman, my father says. Having a lovely time. Wish you were here.

I'm an old sexist, he thinks.

You were a young sexist too, his imaginary daughter says. It was fun, no?

How could I not have been? he says. Don't castigate.

263

I'm not castigating, she says.

We didn't know any better, he says.

Dog ate your homework, she says.

Be quiet, he says. I'm busy.

Doing what? she says.

Trying to get to the lemonness of lemons, he says.

Because somewhere in this moment of the story of a man, a man who could be dead but isn't, who is standing instead at a fruit bay in a supermarket looking at the complexion of lemons grown somewhere, shipped from somewhere to somewhere, driven to here, unloaded into these basins and now on sale here for use before they rot – there's a moral.

But he still can't get to it.

His eyes go from the loose ones in the tub to the bay of lemons bagged in the yellow plastic netting. He picks a lemon up from the loose pile. He holds it in his hand, feels the weight of it. He holds it to his nose. Nothing. He digs the nail of his thumb a little into the skin past the wax and tries again, and there it is, the far high smell of lemon, sweetness and bitterness at once.

Sight, smell and touch, vitality again in so many senses, just from the proximity to a lemon. That's what he should be feeling.

But what's in his head now is the little lemon tree some friend of his ex-wife gave his ex-wife for Christmas, quite near the end, the Christmas before they left him, and it was a spindly thin thing with one single cuckoo-sized lemon growing on it so huge and heavy and bright compared to the thin-stemmed thing that had produced it that it made fruitfulness seem a kind of monster.

That tree had arrived smelling heavenly. Then it lost all its flowers, lost all its leaves, grew leaves again, lost them again, grew a few back again. But it was a resilient thing. It had only finally died the winter after they'd gone and he realized he'd never once thought to water it in all the months.

Well, they grew in the heat, didn't they, in arid countries. They weren't supposed to need water.

None of this is what he wants to be thinking.

He wants to be thinking yes! life! zest!

And a woman! a perfect stranger! who hugged him, who recognized him! knew who he was! said he'd made her day, knew what he'd done in the world! knew his work better than he did!

No.

A leafless tree is what he's thinking.

Would it be a different experience if these lemons weren't supermarket lemons? If they were organic Sicilian lemons with their leaves still attached, instead of mass-produced factory lemons grown in massive greenhouses and sprayed with chemicals? Would it be different if he were in actual Sicily under a warmer sky looking at a lemon still connected to its tree?

He thinks of a fruit tree ruined, by him.

What on earth is he doing?

Above all, right now, what on earth is he doing here, in some alien part of the country where the people speak their English with such strange pure vowels as they walk round and past him, him coming down from a high after the deepest low in his life, the low still there under him, a pit camouflaged for a while by the few spindly wilting branches of something else happening, and under it all, still there, his friend still dead, his family still gone, his work still in shreds, a fruit tree ruined forever, his life a winter desert?

1.34 on the supermarket clock.

Above the heads of everyone in the place the supermarket is playing a song telling everyone to reach for stars and climb high mountains.

Come on, Mr Drama, his imaginary daughter says. You so-called king of the arts. What on earth are you doing? What are you doing on earth?

He looks at the lemon in his hand.

Then he sees, beyond his own hand, what's her name, Britt, the security guard.

She is running up and down the fruit aisle. He sees her rush out through the front entrance and stand there, then rush back in again and sprint along the backs of the cashiers and the scanning area.

She is running like a lunatic. She is as frantic as the song playing above all their heads. She sees him.

She runs at him. She is shouting.

Are they? she says.

I'm sorry? he says.

With you? she says. Are they with you?

Who? he says.

Where are they? she says. Did you see where they went? When did you last see them?

With you, in the car park, he says. Ten minutes ago.

Are you lying? she says. Are you in on it?

What? he says. On what? They'll be in the truck.

He comes out into the car park with her. They go to where he thought the coffee truck was parked, but they can't find the right row of vehicles. Or it's gone.

It was here, she shouts.

She stands in a gap between a couple of four-by-fours.

It was *here*, she shouts. It was *here*.

She is almost wailing. She is swinging a pink duffel bag about in the air where the truck was, hitting it repeatedly off the side of one of the four-by-fours. An alarm goes off in the car she hits. She doesn't notice.

You don't understand, she says. I've got her schoolbag. She'll need this bag. It's a matter of trust. I can't believe she did this. I can't believe she'd do this.

They can't have gone far, he says. Call them on your phone.

She doesn't have a phone, she wails.

They were going to the battlefield, he says. Take a taxi. Call a taxi company.

The security guard gets her phone out.

She asks him the name of the battlefield again.

It is not until much later in the afternoon, after the battlefield, after the SA4A vans, after the shouting and the police, after it's all over and he is standing trying to put it together in his head, amazed at his own lack of ability to see what's happening right in front of his eyes, that he puts his hand in his jacket pocket and finds there the lemon he'd been holding in his hand and looking for some kind of moral in, in the fruit aisle of the supermarket.

That was October.

It's now next March.

By now Richard knows the road between Inverness and Culloden quite well, having gone back and fore, as people say up here, so many times interviewing for his new project, the film he's planning to call A Thousand Thousand People.

Dear Martin,
Apologies.
I can't make your film for you.
vbw
R.

He is filming people in silhouette, for anonymity. He films them in the coffee truck parked in the battlefield car park for atmosphere. He arrives, gets the little camera out and ready on its stick, the interviewees arrive, they sit on the low stool inside the truck below the price list for coffees that never existed, he gets the light right so that there's no way anyone's visual identity can be made use of by anyone else, and he presses the button.

Recording.

Don't the people you've filtered through here become very conspicuous in a village or small town where every stranger will be noticed? he says to his first interviewee.

We're a countrywide network, the silhouette that's the shape of Alda, the woman who drove the coffee truck that day he first came here himself, will say. But it's good here too. There's a lot of tourism. And for the most part, folk here are kind. And if anyone's abrasive, well, if you've crossed the world already and survived, got yourself all the way here under God knows what duress, then any local abrasion, wherever you are, is likely to feel like nothing more than midges.

Alda isn't her real name.

She won't tell him her real name.

Everyone in the Auld Alliance network calls herself or himself by the name Alda or Aldo Lyons.

When he first sent an email to the original Alda care of the library in Kingussie, someone forwarded it to her and she wrote back to tell him how their network got its name.

When I was fifteen, she wrote, and had seen your Andy Hoffnung on TV and loved it, I found the

Beethoven song An Die Hoffnung on a cassette.
I listened to it. I even went to the library and looked
up the German words and worked out what they
meant with a German dictionary. Then I got the
train through to Aberdeen, where they had copies
of The Listener in the stacks, and I looked up what
your friend Paddy said when they interviewed her
about writing Andy Hoffnung, and why she'd
called it that.

And I loved how she'd made the song name
become the man's name. I loved how she made
words that mean *dedicated to hope* into an actual
person, how she gave the words a human shape.

You claim, he says in one of the interviews, that
you've so far helped 235 people escape or outwit
detention estate. Are you exaggerating?

I think it's actually substantially more than 235,
the silhouette says.

This silhouette, who calls herself Alda Lyons like
the others, is one of the people originally helped by
Auld Alliance and who now in turn works for Auld
Alliance helping other people.

Don't think for a minute any of it is easy, she says
to camera. It is truly very difficult.

She speaks beautifully, in a thoughtful and hard-
won English.

Difficult how? he says.

What it means is, she says. We move from one

invisibility to another. I had no rights. I still have no rights. I carried fear on my shoulders all the way across the world to this country you call yours. I still carry the fear on my shoulders. Now I see it like this. Fear is one of my belongings. Fear will always be a part of any belonging, anywhere, that I ever do, for the rest of my life. I fought hard, to get here to your country. And the first thing you did when I arrived was hand me a letter saying, *Welcome to a country in which you are not welcome. You are now a designated unwelcome person with whom we will do as we please.* Never mind the hundred battles I'd fought to get here. This was the lowest time for my soul. And that's the very time at which my battle really began. But I've been lucky. I was helped. There are different ways to be a nobody. There are different kinds of invisibility. Some are more equal than others. I'm speaking, as you British say, from the mouth of the horse.

It's a vicious circle, though, Richard says when he interviews the original coffee truck Alda. You're disappearing people from a system which has already disappeared them.

Alda laughs.

To recoin a phrase, she says. We're letting people take back control of their own hegemony.

How? he says.

Via a system of Auld Alliance network members

all over this country from Thurso to Truro who are working for, not against, the people that other people have designated invisible, she says. It's a circle, yes. But there's nothing vicious in it.

What you're doing's not feasible in any real world scenario, Richard says.

It's human, she says. There's no scenario more real. I mean, if we're talking humans in the real world.

Emergency help, he says to one silhouette who calls himself Aldo and arrives with his springer spaniel wet from the sea, which trails sand from Nairn beach all through the coffee truck and lies down with its head on its paws through the interview smelling of wet dog.

It isn't permanent help, Richard says. Surely it does as much damage as good.

Any help is a help, Aldo says, reaching down to pat his dog's head. Eh, Aldo? (Even the dog has an alias.)

But that's not true, Richard says.

Wait till you ever need help, Aldo (the man) says.

Tell us, Richard says, where some of the people you've helped filter out of detention estate are now.

Every anonymous Alda/Aldo he asks shrugs or shakes a head.

What's the monetary benefit for you from this? he asks each person.

Every Alda/Aldo laughs like he's said something funny.

Where do you get your money from to make this network possible? he asks each person.

They shake their shadow-heads.

The original Alda tells him off camera one evening, don't be silly. Use your eyes. We're voluntary. Everyone does what they can. Everyone can do something useful. We share skills. It doesn't take much. It doesn't ask much. There's always more to go round. We're resourceful. There's always a way. Look at you, finding the money for this film by selling off the stuff from your past. On the one hand an old Chinese plate and a tapestry, on the other, A Thousand Thousand People.

Richard has told her about him raising enough money to make this film, and repay the money on the contract he's broken for another project he was working on, by raiding his parents' old things, in storage, in crates untouched for well over a decade, and finding many things people are happily paying him real money for.

But what happens when that resource runs out? he says. This model can't work for long.

Sometimes it doesn't work full stop, she says. Sometimes it goes really wrong. But we sort it. We generally find other resources. One of us remortgaged a house recently. That cut us some slack. When it runs out we'll think again.

We know how lucky we are. We spread our luck around. We're organized.

What about the police? he says. The security firms?

We're breaking no law, she says. It's not against the law, so far anyway, to help people who need help. And even if and when they find ways to say what we're doing is illegal, no difference. We'll still do it. Volunteers all across the country. Countrywide we're trying to change the impossible, to move things an inch at a time all those thousands of miles towards the possible, and believe me, there are a thousand thousand people, to borrow your title, ready to help.

More truthfully? he says. More like thirty five of you, rather than a thousand thousand?

Well, we're still new, she says. We're just getting going. But a lot of people really don't like the way that other people are being treated. A lot of people want to do something to remedy it.

People can't live under the radar any more, he says.

And yet so many do, she says.

People can't have unrecorded lives any more, he says.

We're working to make the act of recording lives different, she says. You know we are. You are too. That's why you're here recording me.

He shakes his head.

Even so, what you're doing's impossible, he says. A pipe dream. They'll smash it in a minute. This is a story for children. A fairy story.

It is, she says. You're right. We *are* a fairy story. We're a folk tale. I don't mean to sound in the least fey. Those stories are deeply serious, all about transformation. How we're changed by things. Or made to change. Or have to learn to change. And that's what we're working on, change. We're serious, too.

She pours him another whisky out of the bottle in the cupboard in the coffee truck, the floor of which they're both sitting on now in the dusk spring light.

Did you have this bottle in the truck that day we drove up here? he says.

The only beverage on the premises, she says.

Could've done with it that day, he says.

Quite a day, she says. People don't usually come to us the way you first encountered us. That girl's mother. People don't usually get out again after the system's swallowed them. You experienced an aberration that day. But then, sometimes there's an improbability, a moment against the odds, and the door opens, the thinnest of cracks. We helped a whole group of women who that child came to the aid of. God knows how she did, I mean, what are the chances? They're the chances. That's what they are. You try not to miss them. A missed chance, a ruined life.

But I don't know how that kid got her mother, or those other women, out of where they were. I don't understand it. Above all I don't understand for the life of me, none of us can, why she'd think it a good idea to bring SA4A here with her like she did. Like explicit sacrifice.

I thought they were friends, family, he says.
I thought you were just being friendly, giving some people a lift, like you were giving me a lift too.
And can I ask –

Ask away, she says.

Do you know yet what happened? he says. To the child, and the mother? I met the girl with no idea what was happening. So preoccupied with my own drama. But that girl, carrying such a weight. The weight of her own story, and even so. Stopping like she did to help me with mine.

Alda shakes her head.

We don't know the end of that story, she says.

He has the Holiday Inn pen in his inside jacket pocket.

He will keep it in the inside pocket of every jacket or coat he wears for the rest of his life.

Five years from now, when he eventually tracks down the girl, Florence, now a young woman, the first thing he'll do is take it out of his inside jacket pocket and show her.

*

But first there are more imminent futures to navigate.

Like this one.

An envelope arrives at Richard's flat. It comes from a solicitor's office. There's an old book in it wrapped in tissue paper.

Its letter tells Richard its contents have been left to him in the last will and testament of the late Patricia Heal.

Collected Stories of Katherine Mansfield. Constable. 1948. Blue hardback, the gold lettering faded and gappy on the spine. Post-war paper, ration-era, yellowed, thin, rough to the touch. Handwriting on the inside front page, a girl's. Patricia Hardiman.

For a couple of weeks just having it there on the table and seeing it every day as he moves about the room is enough.

One afternoon he opens the book near the front at random. He reads a funny, acrid story about middle-class people having a dinner party. The people are ludicrous, fragile, full of themselves and their self-importance, the stories they're making up to themselves about their lives. Meanwhile in the garden of the house there's a pear tree, in full blossom. It stands there laden with flowers, stunningly lovely, nothing to do with any of the people who look at it, or admire it, or think anything about it, or don't even notice it, nothing to do with their realities and their delusions, their conquests and their failures, the knowledge or the naiveties of the people in the house who think they can own that tree.

What a great story.

It's as he's closing the book and he turns it over in his hands that he sees for the first time the pages covered in handwriting at the back.

It is Paddy's handwriting.

He sees his name in her voice.

Hello Doubledick.

The handwriting is her later life handwriting. It starts on the inside back cover and continues for all six and a bit blank pages between the cover and the text, right up to the last page of the last story of the book, the book's final words, in block capitals, THE END.

He get up. He pours himself a drink.

He sits down and opens that book at its end.

Hello Doubledick.

Snow is general all over Ireland, and London too, by God.

Cold feet, you said as you went today.

(Don't say I never listen to you.)

When I got my first pay packet, 1948, for my first week's work as dogsbody at London Films while they launched their Bonnie Prince Charlie, big flop, more's the pity, I went direct to Foyles on Charing Cross Rd.

First thing I ever bought for myself with my own money, this book.

Yours now.

Here's some research for your April.

Katherine Mansfield first, of course, who made a promise to her friend and loyal partner Ida Baker one day. When I die I'll prove there's no afterlife to you, she said, and Ida says how? and Katherine says, After I'm dead I'll send you a coffin worm in a matchbox.

She says it because she knows it'll make soft hearted Ida shriek and shriek, and it does, she squeals I don't want you to send me a worm, so Katherine M says to her, okay, not a worm I promise, I'll send you an earwig in a matchbox instead.

So. A few months later Katherine Mansfield has died, as we do. Her friend is grief stricken. She gets to a cottage she's staying in somewhere or other, it's a few weeks after Katherine M has died, and Ida's dog-tired and sad and cold, and she goes to light the gas to make a pot of tea, picks up the matchbox and there are no matches in it.

But there's something in it all right.

She opens it.

Earwig.

Rilke, now, he had a couple of afterlives that are a whole other matchbox of earwigs.

A countess called Nora was working on

*translations into English from German of the late
Rilke's elegies. She'd exchanged letters with Rilke
about spiritualism in the years before his death (as
opposed to after it, ha ha). So she thinks it'll be a
good idea to go to see a medium, quite a famous
one, and get to meet the dead Rilke in person.*

*And the medium says is there anybody there, and
the letters on the ouija board spell out R I L, and
yes it's the dead man himself come all the way up
from the underworld to tell Countess Nora that he
wants to work with her on her translations.*

*So the dead Rilke and the countess meet at a few
seances and he tells her which words and phrases
he wants changed in her versions.*

*Then he congratulates her on how close to his
originals her English poems are, and tells her how
honoured he's been to work with her.*

Hmm.

*I prefer this kind of uncanny myself: you and I
were just talking today about how they lived so
close to each other, Katherine M and him, and
never met, or if they did probably never knew they
did. But after you went I was online having a
browse for you and I found a letter that Rilke
wrote, he was still in Sierre in Switzerland, and the
letter is dated 10 Jan 23, which is the day after the
day Katherine M dies in Fontainebleau, France.*

*He is writing to a friend in it about how much
he's been moved by reading some D H Lawrence in*

German, the novel The Rainbow. He loves it, he says, and reading it has opened a whole new chapter in his life.

Now, I know that Katherine M was good friends with Lawrence and his wife Frieda, and one day she'd confided in them some stories of her own erotic times when she was younger. And something very close to her own stories of her life – I mean close enough to make her very irate when she read it herself – definitely slipped into one of the characters in The Rainbow.

So guess who Rilke finally met? In fictional form, at least.

Now I've only one more afterlife for you, and I know I'll annoy you Doubledick with this final life after death. Sometimes I talk about Chaplin just to watch you so sweetly pretending it means nothing to you that I'm talking about him.

But there's a strange afterlife connection between Charlie Chaplin and Rilke. There's a sort of connection with Katherine M too, who called her cat Charlie Chaplin, and then that cat chanced to have a couple of litters of kittens, which gave her quite a surprise, the first time anyway. (And I think one of those first kittens of Charlie Chaplin the cat might even have been named – April.)

In the 1930s Charlie Chaplin is visiting St Moritz. He makes some well-heeled new friends, an Egyptian businessman and his wife, a lovely clever *woman called Nimet. One night at dinner Chaplin takes a napkin off the table and ties it round the beautiful Nimet's head like she has terrible toothache. Then he pretends to be a dentist taking out a tooth, and he holds the tooth up, a lump of sugar out of the sugar bowl.*

Now, I'm pretty sure this Nimet is the same beautiful Egyptian woman Rilke picked the roses for, the day the rose thorn pricked his finger with the fairy-tale real-life consequence.

My beloved Chaplin. He moved to Switzerland for good, you know, in the 1950s, when the US threw him out for being too bolshevik and for telling the workers some truths about the machine age in Modern Times. He bought a grand house and grounds, only about an hour away these days from the place Rilke and Mansfield had lived 30 years earlier. He used to come out of his house and shake his fists at the Swiss army practising their gunfire in the valleys and the mountains round his new estate.

He's got a ghost or two wandering the world – one particularly lucrative haunting is the one making money for the Hollywood bar owner who says Chaplin still regularly visits a booth in his bar that used to be reserved for him.

But my own favourite of the Chaplin afterlives is the adventure his own mortal remains went on after he died.

Do you remember how his coffin was dug up from its grave and stolen? This is forty years ago, when we were still young. He died in the December and they stole him in the March. The police told the journalists, like something out of the bible, <u>*The grave is empty! The coffin is gone!*</u> It was missing from March till May, with a great number of fraudsters phoning the Chaplin family all the time asking for money and promising the return of the body, before the police caught two mechanics, dirt poor, political refugees. They'd dug him up, taken a photo of the coffin covered in mud, loaded it into the back of their old car and rattled it a mile down the road from where he last lived, where they buried it in a farmer's cornfield.

The silent remains of the silent star.

Quiet as the grave, in a grave that's not a grave, on what's his 89th birthday in the middle of April 1978, under the earth under the green shoots under the birdsong under the air under the cold spring sky.

Expect the unexpected afterlives, Doubledick. Life goes on.

For today, I hope you dried those socks and shoes. For tomorrow, may your feet always be warm, old friend.

Your own,
your ever,
your earwig,
P.

Then her handwriting ends, round the words printed in the book,

THE END

and just above these there's the text of the last story in the book, ending with the lines:

"God! what a woman you are," said the man. "You make me so infernally proud – dearest, that I . . . I tell you!"

and Paddy has written an annotation with an arrow pointing to these last lines.

Proud of you, Doubledick. Blaze the trail. Make it your film, not his film.

In a break between interviews one sunny rainy day in that first spring after Paddy, he walks to the place called Clava about a mile down the road from the battlefield car park.

At Clava there's a gathering of ancient burial cairns from 4,000 years ago, tombs that would at one point have been ten feet high, roofed and dark. The burial mounds are now just rings of stones wide open to the sky. They're made of circles of piled-up large and small stones, with a cohort of standing stones round them like they're keeping watch on the tombs.

It's spring but it's cold. He chooses the tomb most in the sun. He goes down its stone passageway. He stands in a grave and looks up at the clouds.

There's nothing at all left of whoever was once

buried here. There's nothing here but piles of stone, trodden path, grass scattered with daisies and clover, bare spring trees whose trunks are bright green with the damp and the moss, above his head an occasional bird call.

Richard walks out of the tomb.

(That's something you can't say every day.)

There's nobody else visiting Clava today. Good. That's lucky. He's been warned how busy it can be.

He's been told, too, how a few years ago a tourist from Belgium helped himself to one of these stones, picked it up and took it home with him. A few months later the Inverness Tourist Office received a stone in the post and a map of the place he'd taken it from in Clava. Please put this stone back, the enclosed letter said. My daughter's broken a leg, my wife is really unwell, I myself have lost my job and broken an arm. Please apologize to the spirit of the place from which I took this stone.

Respect.

Richard stands in the grass and clay, next to a leaning old boulder.

Just to let you know, Pad, he says. Knowing how much you love Chaplin. I'm told by the locals that just down the road from here there's a house he actually owned late in his life, and he and his family used to come here for holidays. He's probably been here too and had a look round the place.

And also. I'm somatizing. This project's making me feel, all right. It's making me feel very all right. I'm spending all this time in a place I don't know, and I feel like I'm home. I meet people all the time who are risking themselves and they fill me with their confidence. I don't belong, they know I don't, I know I don't. But I feel like I do. What I feel is welcome.

I'm having an unexpectedly lovely time. I wish you were here.

He has the poem in his pocket. He takes it out and unfolds it in the sharp sunlight. The Cloud, by Percy Bysshe Shelley; this is its last verse.

> *I am the daughter of Earth and Water,*
> *And the nursling of the Sky;*
> *I pass through the pores of the oceans and*
> *   shores;*
> *I change, but I cannot die.*
> *For after the rain when with never a stain*
> *The pavilion of Heaven is bare,*
> *And the winds and sunbeams with their*
> *   convex gleams*
> *Build up the blue dome of air,*
> *I silently laugh at my own cenotaph,*
> *And out of the caverns of rain,*
> *Like a child from the womb, like a ghost from*
> *   the tomb,*
> *I arise and unbuild it again.*

*

Unbuilding, undying, the cloud of unknowing, changing its shape as it crosses the sky.

The unexpected afterlives.

Quite often after that autumn day when his life ended so it could begin again, Richard will think back to those cloud and mountain pictures, remember, the ones he saw in London at the Royal Academy in the early summer of 2018, the pictures made of slate and chalk.

One day around Christmas time, in a round-up of the year's best exhibitions in one of the papers, he reads an article called A Postcard to Tacita.

In it, there's a story of how, one day in the gallery, a small child, two or three years old, threw herself at one of the pictures in the exhibition and smudged its chalk.

The artist tells the interviewer that she doesn't like to put those little low wire barriers between the pictures she makes and the people looking at them, and not just because people are actually more likely to trip over them than not. She doesn't want anything to be between the person and the picture. But sometimes people and pictures too literally collide. If they get damaged, the artist says, the pictures can be repaired so long as whatever hits them or smudges them isn't wet. Though *when someone shook an umbrella in New York*, well. Those raindrops are now a part of the picture they hit, and will be for as long as the picture exists.

Richard laughs out loud at the thought of the child throwing herself at the picture. He hopes it was the mountain she threw herself at.

Then he remembers the young woman he stood next to for half a minute in the gallery that day looking at the mountain.

Fuck me.

Fuck me too.

His daughter will be about that woman's age now.

His daughter is a girl he last saw in the year 1987, February, the day she sat on his knee and he read one of her books to her. Beatrix Potter. The good rabbit's carrot was stolen by the bad rabbit. But the hunter chased the bad rabbit till there was nothing left of it but a rabbit tail on a bench.

She laughed and laughed at the picture of the fluffy white tail on the bench.

He puts the Sunday paper in the recycling. He comes back and sits at the table. He opens the laptop.

He types his daughter's name into the search engine. He takes his time over each letter of her name.

He has never done this before.

He has never dared.

He has told himself she wouldn't want him to.

Hers is a slightly unusual name, same spelling as his mother's with the s instead of z in Elisabeth, and if she kept her own mother's name or isn't married, a quite uncommon surn –

It comes straight up, a picture of a woman who will be her.

It is surely her.

It is definitely her.

There are several pictures. She looks like her mother in one, and like his mother in another.

She works at a university in London. There is an email address.

Do I dare?

I don't.

She won't, wouldn't, want me to.

He leaves the room.

He walks all round the flat.

He comes back into the room.

Thinking her dead, dead to me, dead to my world, all these years, he says inside his head that night, wide awake in bed, middle of the night, staring at the old ceiling rose he's never noticed before though he's lived here all the years.

His imaginary daughter laughs.

What are you like? she says inside his head.

What are you like? he says inside his head to his real daughter.

Silence.

Yeah but enough about the filmmaker and what Russell would call the zzzzzzzz of his story – back to Brit six months ago in October, in the van with Florence and two total strangers on a backroad fuck knows where, going further north, at least Brit thinks it's north. She watches, like a detective on TV or a person in a drama who's being kidnapped, for roadsigns with the names of places on them, in case it will be important.

This woman is the world's worst driver.

There are two seatbelts and currently four people in the front of this van being driven by someone who doesn't seem bothered about how unsafe it is to have so many people crammed in the front of a joke of a vehicle with a fancy fake-foreign interior as if that'll make up for having no road weight at all.

Brit has given up her own seatbelt for Florence,

who's squashed over against the door but at least belted in. If they crash it's Brit and the man who'll go through the windscreen.

The man is called Richard.

The Scotch woman is called Alda, like Aldi the shop. She and Brit had a stand-up fight at the station.

– *SA4A in my van? I don't think so.*

– *I go where she goes.*

– *(to Florence) What've you brought a SA4A goon here for? What are you playing at? This isn't a game.*

– *How dare you threaten her. How dare you call me a goon.*

– *She's not SA4A. She's Brittany, my friend. (Florence)*

– *It says SA4A. Look. Right there on her jacket.*

– *It's okay. I trust her. (Florence)*

Florence trusts her. But Winner of World's Worst Driver 2018 is making her driving even more terrifying by swivelling about in the driver's seat looking at things in the scenery and pointing them out. She is giving her filmmaker friend some historic-tour prattle about the area, on which she is clearly some kind of expert.

It's not like Brit isn't trying to join in.

She is not stupid. She knows some history, and a lot of things about films too.

She knows about, she has known, too, people who have died, including her own father.

She drops in the thing she looked up yesterday about Cassandra the legendary fortune-teller of the future who the gods cursed by making what she said never make any difference to anyone who heard it, even though it was true.

She is not brainless.

Word in edgewise?

No one will let her.

Are you a director? Brit says to the man when they finally stop talking to each other for a minute.

The man tells her that he worked for TV when he was younger, making the kind of TV that a lot of people didn't really approve of. He says he's working on a film now about poets who lived hundreds of years ago and that it's set in Switzerland and is a historical drama. He says probably they're too young to have seen something he made on TV but if they have that they'll probably have completely forgotten it. All the same, he says, if they saw it, then it'll be inside them, because everything we see goes somewhere into our memories and is in there even though we don't know it's there.

That is so true, Brit says. The most really unforgettable thing I ever saw on a film was on TV. Sometimes if it comes into my head at night even now and I'm in bed, I can't sleep. I won't sleep all night. It isn't even that horrible, or that graphic. I've actually seen so many more things that are so much more graphic on TV and in films. And in real life. I see every day in my job things you'd be much more sure would mark you for life. Even if you didn't see them in real life and only saw them in a film.

But they don't, not like this one. I can't forget it. Maybe you'll know it, it's the one of a man in a courtroom, I mean it really happened, it's really happening, it's not just a drama.

He's being shouted at and made fun of by a judge, a bigshot Nazi judge who's shouting at this guy standing at the front of the court and there's an audience watching in the courtroom too. And the judge is giving him this really big dressing-down. And the thing is, the man, a soldier, has had his uniform taken off him and obviously been given a pair of trousers way too big for him and no belt to tie them up with so he has to hold them up all the time or they'll fall down. And this means that when he has to do things with his arms and hands like saluting and holding a book it's awkward to, and they keep giving him things like that to do.

It's supposed to be funny. You're supposed to be laughing at him. And the judge is calling him a traitor and shouting at him about his treachery and making fun of him, and the man sort of stammers and speaks up for himself like he thinks explaining will help. Like, he's an idiot. He's got no idea. He just keeps on going, he says but this isn't what we should be doing, we were just standing shooting people into these pits we'd made them dig, this isn't fighting, it isn't right, it is wrong, stuff like that.

And the judge makes fun of him some more and then pronounces the death sentence, and presumably they took him out then and there and shot him in the head in the courtyard.

But what got me about it, and what gets me when I think about it, is that they were taking this film of it at all. Because in the end it was all for the camera. All of it. It wasn't about justice, or there not being justice. Well, it was, on one level. It was about who was in charge of justice, who gets to say what it is. But really. Really it was made for the people who were watching it. Like they were meant, the audience that was there in the courtroom but also all the people everywhere who'd be seeing that film, to find it really funny and at the same time they were meant to be scared by it. They weren't meant to think, oh that's so unfair, or, look at the way that man's being used or treated, like we can see now. Well, they were too, but only because it's what could happen to *them*. But most of all they were meant to laugh at him and then to learn from it how to behave, like what *not* to do, and to know what would happen to them if they ever did what they weren't meant to.

I was about her age when I saw it. I didn't sleep for days on end. You know that piece of film? You ever see it?

But the filmmaker next to her just laughs.

He starts talking about doing your best and being good-humoured.

I don't see that there was much chance for him to be good-humoured about anything with the Nazis about to shoot him in the head, Brit says.

The filmmaker says Nazi stuff shouldn't be on TV so much, and then goes on about how playing old songs on the radio is wrong. Then he starts talking about horses.

Thanks anyway. For the sheer banality of your observations, Brit says.

My pleasure, the man says.

Brit gives him a look like he's a constant watch case.

He asks Florence if she's okay so squashed up against the side of the van.

I'm doing my best in a bad situation and staying good-humoured about it, she says.

Everybody laughs.

Think you're funny, Brit says.

I *am* funny, Florence says.

Funny in the head, Brit says.

She nudges Florence. She nods towards the filmmaker.

**Seconds after she says that funny in the head thing
she starts to feel bad about having said it.**

She is questioning everything she is doing so
much, about whether it is right or wrong, that she
is beginning to wonder if she is going a bit mad.

Then the woman driving them decides to drive
them *all* mad by singing songs, in a language.

First she tells them the story of the song she's
going to sing, about an empty house next to a lake,
and some ghosts of people who once lived there and
were made to leave it when landlords burned them
out are sitting in the snow on what was their floor
where their fireplace was and their beds once were,
and they are looking up through the place where
the roof once was at a sky with no stars and
no moon.

Then it turns out that they're not ghosts at all,

they're real people sitting in that snow, and that now they're across the sea in Canada and can't stop thinking of the time they sat in the snow in what had once been their house.

Then she starts singing the story in a foreign language.

It is what Josh would call *keeping it surreal*. It is what Russell would call wankbag. She casts a glance at Florence while the woman sings the weird way that sounds like someone both caressing you and accusing you. She makes a face at Florence about the singing as if to say *weird*.

Then she feels bad for doing that too.

The filmmaker has fallen asleep and is leaning really heavily on Brit. The woman starts to sing another sad sounding song. She tells them, like she's speaking to an audience somewhere and not just some people she's driving, one of whom is asleep and isn't listening anyway, that this next song is about a person who goes hillwalking and who starts to be followed by the sound of his own footsteps, but much louder and larger sounding than the footprints his own boots are making in the snow. And when he looks round he finds he's being followed by a huge grey man, called The Grey Man, out in just his shirtsleeves in the snow, who disappears as soon as the clouds shift above the mountain.

Like a ghostly presence, Florence says.

His own shadow, Brit says.

The woman stops halfway through her singing to tell them that the people who go up those mountains over there, walking or climbing, quite often really do hear the sound of someone else's footsteps behind them –

yeah,

right,

– and that this is why the song got written. She tells them there's a local rumour that it's the ghost of a man called William the Smith who was a local poet and philosopher and poacher, but that the song suggests it's the sound of the footsteps of all the people anywhere in the world who've been wronged, and in its last verse, which she'll sing them in a minute, the song says we're all followed by the sound of these footsteps wherever we go, but it's only in the mountains or the countryside, away from the hurly burly of the town and the noise of ourselves, that we can hear the true size of what lies behind our own footsteps.

So it's just as well, then, Brit thinks, that it's being sung in a secret language and nobody has to be bothered by such patronizing garbage being in English and having to actually consider it even for a split second.

The woman starts back into singing the song again like they're stuck in some awful olden times pub.

William the Smith, Florence says. I am from now on going to choose to be known as Florence the Smith. Poet and philosopher and poacher. What's a poacher?

Someone who poaches eggs, Brit says.

Someone who charms the deer and the fish that don't belong to him or her right into his or her hands with just one look, the woman says.

Brit laughs.

Florence the Smith. You said it. That's you. She's Florence the Smith all right, Brit says.

She has had enough of being an armrest now for the filmmaker, who smells too much of old man. She nudges her arm and her shoulder into him really hard as if the van's taken a corner.

It wakes him up.

He shifts over.

Result.

But then he and the woman driving start talking only to each other again and as if they're actually into each other or something. You'd have thought they were both well past it at their age, he looks ancient, talk about Grey Man. She's fifty if she's anything, embarrassing, distasteful at that age, and it's like Brit and Florence aren't even here in this van –

her: *think I know a really good place for you to say goodbye to your friend blah blah a really ancient place standing stones ancient place of burial really beautiful* him: *sounds like it might be exactly right*

her: *except it's got a tendency to be busy since they started making Outlander*

him: *what's Outlander*

her: *TV series all about time travelling you don't know Outlander wow everybody knows Outlander where've you been blah inspired by Clava so many cars now it's hard to get home sometimes or get parked outside your own house and now people go there to have seances to try to raise characters that have died in Outlander*

him: *seances to contact dead fictional characters*

her: *aye I know*

(Laughter)

him: *does it work do the fictional characters send them messages from character heaven*

her: *I have no idea*

him: *she'd love that she'd have loved that that whole thing it'd make her laugh and say something very philosophical about human nature and then she'd probably go and make a list of all the characters she'd like to ask questions herself then go there and do it blah amazing really seances to talk to dead fictional characters*

her: *only in the highlands eh where we welcome everybody a hundred thousand welcomes that's our motto a warm welcome even to ghosts aye even to the ghosts of the imagined*

him: *you're a very versatile people*

her: *right enough*

(Laughter)

him: *beautiful haunting songs I'm assuming you're a native speaker*

her: *no I went to evening class I wanted to learn a language my own family spoke two centuries ago and then were made to stop speaking not that it's a dead language it's thriving blah didn't choose it at school partly because it was too much work sounded too difficult blah courses five years and now I can sing in it which is a start*

— at least thank God the creepy singing, in the language that sounds like nothing Brit has ever heard in her life (even in Spring House with all its languages, and it is a horrible feeling when you can't speak a language and aren't in charge of or superior to the person who's speaking it, who might be saying anything at all and you haven't a fucking clue and no right to tell them to be quiet or choose to ignore them), has stopped.

At least the songs about things like your own footsteps following you wherever you go and being so much bigger than you are finished.

Children born up here in this country growing up hearing stuff like that must be freaked out all the time.

Or if not then they must be incredibly well adjusted when unbelievable things happen to them.

At least now too Brit has stopped feeling bad herself.

She has been quite surprised by how unpleasant she is to other people without even thinking, and by how bad her being unpleasant to other people is currently making her feel.

But she's the only person in this van who's really got Florence's back. It is lucky Brit is here. No one else is even noticing, except Brit. While the singing was happening Florence's whole self was *like a coiled spring*, what Torq says in his gay way when he's trying to describe people who are tense. Now they're talking about some music machine from the past and nobody has noticed that Florence is getting more and more nervy.

Even so, Florence says the nice thing about her when the man is telling the story of the inventor of the machine. She says,

Brittany's an inventor too, she has really good ideas for making things.

They aren't listening to her and don't hear her. But Brit hears her say it.

Last night in the Holiday Inn, before she goes to her own room, Brit gives Florence some of the chocolate she got for them both out of the machine in the corridor and makes sure everything's all right for her in the room she's been given.

Anything you need? Want me to tell you a bedtime story? she says.

She is half serious. That's what you're meant to do, isn't it, when you settle a kid to sleep.

Get with the nearly adolescent programme, Brittany, Florence says.

Your loss, Brit says.

Loss of what? And how? Florence says.

Of me telling you a bedtime story. You'll never know, now, ever, the story I would've told you, Brit says.

Actually, I have a story for you, Florence says. No, not so much a story. More a question.

I'm listening, Brit says.

What is refugee chic? Florence says.

I don't know, Brit says. Is this a trick question?

No, Florence says. I seriously want to know what it is.

Is it a band? Brit says.

It's words I saw on the floor of the bus, Florence says. It was on the front of one of those magazines that come with the newspapers at the weekend. It was a picture of some people wearing clothes, and the words on it were Refugee Chic. And I was thinking about it because, considering that I am already worrying about getting up tomorrow morning with no clean change of underwear, I have begun to wonder what it would be like to never know what was going to happen to you next, or to have no way of getting yourself clean or of knowing whether you'd have a clean place to rest, before it all started again the next day.

You trying to get round me with all this lefty hand-wringing talk? Brit says.

Florence shrugs her eyes.

Or is this a manipulative attempt to get me to wash out some clothes for you? Brit says. Because you're twelve. Which is too old for a bedtime story and old enough to wash your own. Do it now and hang them in there on the radiator with the towels on it. They'll dry by tomorrow.

I'm just asking. What is it? Florence says again. What is refugee chic?

Brit turns her back to the girl, leans against the TV desk, puts her hands over her own face like there's something she doesn't want to see.

I have no fucking idea what I'm doing here, she says.

You're my private security guard, Florence says. You're keeping me SA4A. SA4A with you, SA4A for you, SA4A together.

Those are SA4A straplines. They're on the posters all through the centre telling anyone who reads them about SA4A's policy of equal treatment for all regardless of gender, race or religion.

You are taking the piss out of me, Brit says still with her hands over her eyes. Don't you dare. Don't you dare make fun of me.

I'm not, Florence says. I wouldn't. I'm just speaking one of our languages.

Why do you even need a private security guard? Brit says. You're fine in the world. You've got it made. You do your thing and it all just opens like fucking flowers for you. You don't need me.

I do, Florence says. Don't you get it? It's the most obvious thing ever.

No, Brit said. I don't get it. Okay?

Brittany, we are humanizing the machine,

Florence says. Get with the humanizing the machine programme

We are? Brit says.

Yes, Florence says. I can't do it without you. Nobody can.

Brit still has her hands over her eyes.

Explain, she says from behind her hands.

Okay, so, Florence says. The machine only works because on the one hand humans make it work and on the other hand humans let it work. Yes? Agreed?

Uh huh, Brit says.

So I thought I'd try employing it direct. Ask it to work for me for a change, Florence says. And it said yes. You said yes.

Oh, Brit says still seeing only the insides of her own hands. And what are you going to pay me for doing this employment that's got absolutely zilcho future prospects for me?

My respects, Florence says. Your dues. Our debt to society.

Think you're so clever with words, Brit says.

I am, Florence says. I'm going to write books. Some day you'll read the book I'll write about you.

Is that a promise or a threat? Brit says.

Florence laughs.

You tell me, machine, she says.

Brit finally turns, takes her hands away from her face, looks straight at Florence.

Cause what I *really* don't get, she says. Why pick

me? Why me and not anyone else getting off my train? There were plenty other SA4A staff on that train. Quite a lot of us on shift change, and they all walked past you this morning too. So why *me*? What was it about *me*? What was it you thought you could tell by just looking at *me* that made you think, yeah, that person, rather than that one, or that one?

Brittany, Florence says.

What? Brit says.

Gelf, Florence says.

What's gelf mean? she says.

Get over yourself, Florence says.

Brit sighs.

Lucky that that's where we're going tomorrow, then, she says.

Where? Florence says.

The place you showed me on the postcard. The gelf course, Brit says.

And you ask me why I chose you, Florence says.

She throws her arms in the air like a comedy presenter on a kids' TV show.

In her own room later Brit lies on the bed flicking channels between a show about pitbulls maybe getting put down or maybe getting saved from legally having to be destroyed, and an episode of The Apprentice where the cretins who've signed up for it are making doughnuts with flavours nobody will ever pay money to eat, just so they can be ritually humiliated in the second half of the episode.

She wonders if she'll get up in the morning to find Florence's room empty and Florence gone.

She knows she won't.

She knows Florence'll be there all right.

An animal in the zoo next to the hotel is making a noise, lowing, to use an old word from history and songs that nobody uses in real life any more. Definitely a word she's never had call herself to use for anything. But it's a good word for it. It sounds low, the noise.

She thinks of all the different kinds of animals just a stone's throw away.

God all fucking mighty. In a minute she'll be wondering what it's really truly like to be a fucking bison or penguin or whatever.

Tell myself a bedtime story, she thinks.

Once there was a Detainee Custody Officer who was on to something. But what? It was mysterious, and at the same time really straightforward. It could cost her her job. Or it might mean a better job. It could be a game changer at work. But it might also be bigger than work. It might be a life changer.

In any case, she couldn't not do it, couldn't not have done it.

She did not have a choice.

She knows now that the story about the sex

house is easily true. That girl in the room along the corridor could definitely easily have walked into the sex house and got right up their noses, making them feel and act like they've never acted before and making them stop what they're doing and open the locked doors and windows and look the other way while all those girls got out of there.

She can picture their stunned faces. She can feel their rage when the typical Florence concussion effect fades enough for them to remember who they are and how much cash has just walked out the door.

But how that kid will have managed to do this without getting raped and killed, and without the protection of a whole army of private security guards, is what Brit can't work out.

There's also a chance that those people who run that place will have been changed by it, and by her – properly changed, changed at life level. Rather than just having an hour's blurred new vision then back to the usual.

Brit imagines them cleaning themselves up, cleaning up the fetid rooms, throwing out the fetid bedstuff, treating with gentleness what girls and women were left in there then letting them go, cleaned up, apologized to, given their cut of the money they've made, off out into the world with something of the freedom those girls and women originally thought they'd have, coming here in the first place.

She switches the TV off.

She gets into the hotel bed.

She thinks in the dark and in the sound of the creature lowing, not an unpleasant sound, not an anxious sound, just a sound she's never heard before, a sound new to her, from an animal letting people and animals know that it's stuck in a zoo and is wondering if anything else anywhere in the neighbourhood speaks its language. It will want to talk about being stuck in a zoo. It will want to say, are there other lives possible for me than this one in here?

The girl is like someone or something out of a legend or a story, the kind of story that on the one hand isn't really about real life but on the other is the only way you ever really understand anything about real life.

She makes people behave like they should, or like they live in a different better world.

Get over yourself.

Brit laughs in the dark.

What is refugee chic.

She's, what's the word?

Another old word from history and songs that nobody uses in real life any more.

She is good.

But this is the point in the story when the girl will pull a fast one after all.

So it isn't, wasn't, goodness.

Or if it is, it's a good that's not and has never really been about Brit anyway.

So fuck that.

They're on their way into a Tesco. They pull into the car park and the woman switches the engine off and they all get out and say goodbye to the filmmaker, and all the way into the shop the woman is talking about her *mother's soup*, listing what they'll need. Leeks, celery, carrots, a big potato, a garlic, some sprigs of thyme.

She's said that phrase *my mother's soup* several times. It may be a coded reference to something to do with Florence's mother, but may also just as well be boring information about the woman's mother making some soup.

This Tesco is like the ones in England. It's one of those big Tescos that even have their own post office. It has a rack of postcards at the front of it, pictures of the place where they are. Brit stops and picks one off the rack, of a cartoon Loch Ness monster in a real lake. She thinks for a minute about sending a postcard. But who would she send it to? Her mother? Stel? Torq? Josh?

Like she's on a holiday.

She thinks it and her usual life enters her like she's been taken over by a live dead thing. She hangs heavy from her own shoulders over Florence at the vegetable racks, turns and hangs over the bags of salad and her shoulders feel as big and as dead to her as the dead person's shoulders look in the old films where a scientist makes a person out of bits of dead people.

Any minute now, though Brit doesn't know it yet, the woman and Florence are going to dodge her.

They'll both go to the ladies' toilet, where there's suddenly quite a queue of women falling in behind them, so that Brit gets blocked and is made to wait outside.

They'll go in and not come out. When she goes in to look they won't be in either of the stalls.

She'll run up and down the supermarket aisles. She'll run outside to the car park.

She'll have gone, the girl will have gone, without taking her schoolbag.

It will feel urgent, that she gets the schoolbag to the girl.

Then she'll despise herself. Because she has been tricked. Because it was never about her. Because she was never a real part of the story.

She was just an extra in it.

She was the hired help.

She'll stand with the filmmaker in the car park at a loss in the space where the van was. In fact Brit will be feeling that word loss like she has never felt it, apart from when she was the girl's age and her father died. The world will tilt. She will stand *at a loss* like a loss is a rail on the side of a ship and what's been lost is somewhere deep in a sea the ship is stuck on the surface of.

Call a taxi, the filmmaker'll be saying.

In a minute, she'll say.

Will I fuck, she will think.

She'll phone the SA4A Countrywide 24-Hour Hotline number.

What's the name of that battlefield again? she'll say as she waits for them to answer.

That was Brit in autumn.

It's spring now. Here's a window (one of the kind that opens) on to DCO Brittany Hall's spring in Spring House IRC, let's choose a late March day, typical Tuesday afternoon.

She's at work on a shift with Russell.

He's laughing like a drain at the empty bowl someone's left outside the Kurdish guy who's on hunger strike's door. He is pretending that Brit ate something then left the bowl outside empty to taunt the Kurdish deet.

She is not finding it funny.

Who was it ate it if you didn't? Russell is saying to Brit. You did, you greedy cunt.

Brit is saying nothing, so as not to annoy Russell. Russell is a dick. But he's her friend in here, isn't he? And you need your friends in here.

There hasn't been promotion.

There's been nothing, nothing from management at all, though Stel will report back to her that she'd heard via the office that SA4A top level were very grateful at the time for her phonecall, particularly because they couldn't get the facial rec tech to work on the girl's face, partly because of angles and age and ethnicity – Stel always gets annoyed that facial rec doesn't work on black people very well, which means people get arrested who aren't the right people, sometimes aren't even the right gender – and partly because the system, for whatever reason, just refused to work.

Also, Stel tells her, it's down to her, and management knows it's down to her, that SA4A and the HO have been able to *identify ringleaders* and are working to shut down a *wannabe underground railroad group* using the railway system at both ends of the country, a network run by cynical activists aiding and abetting illegals for illegal gain, and that her help with this is bound to be on her record for when they look to see who they want to promote.

The woman? The story goes, deported.

But the story also goes, she was picked up, kept in for two months, got let out on indefinite in case of media attention (she's got a story now) and can be picked up again when interest dies down.

The girl? Legally can't be picked up, dep'd or

anything till she's eighteen and legally becomes a citizen, or not, depending on whether she's got legal papers.

Information Brit isn't party to.

Back in October Brit had small gatherings of staff from across the wings crowding round her in the Ladies three times in total, asking her to tell them what happened.

She told them about getting out there to the battlefield in a taxi in time to see the SA4A vans arrive in the car park.

She left out how she watched the uniforms spread out across the landscape and ran off herself in the opposite direction across paths and grass, through tourists on holiday, visitors doing a tour, till she stopped and bent over and was as sick as a dog next to a sign with the words Conservation in Action on it.

What she said is this sort of thing:

I think literally hypnosis. Not just me but several train guards and a woman in the Holiday Inn. I saw it happen to the other people and didn't realize it was happening to me too. Like when Derren Brown can make people do things on TV they've no idea they're doing or why they're doing. Hardly recognized myself. I reckon she hypnotized the facial rec system too. If you can do it to a person I bet she could do it to appliances. I mean a

lot of machines are designed to listen to us.
So, I mean, what if they're <u>really</u> listening to
people?

Cue a lot of jokes about liberal elite toasters, bleeding heart hairdryers, politically correct washing machines.

By her third day back at work people knew the story and stopped being interested. By the fourth not even the deets were asking any more.

She listened one winter night to the song by the person called Noname, the one called Self, that the girl told her was a favourite song.

She was surprised at how obscene some of the lyrics are. There is a lot of bad language in it. A twelve-year-old girl really shouldn't be listening to music like that. That's bad parenting.

After it, the Nina Simone song, about how things are going to get easier, sounded – well, Brit had two images in her head, one of a Disney cat like the ones in the old film The Aristocats, and the other a real cat, the one the boys from the other side of the park superglued to a tree back when Brit was twelve herself.

One Noname line stuck in Brit's head too – the one where she says something about a female cunt writing a thesis about colonialism.

Brit looked up the word colonialism on a web dictionary to remind herself exactly.

A practice of domination, which involves the subjugation of one people to another.

It is a funny image, a cunt writing a thesis at a university. Maybe it means they're all cunts at university, ho ho ho.

But that girl was bright, like close to insane bright. She'd have been one of the cleverest people in her year at her school. Brit still has the Hot Air book, in fact she still has, in her wardrobe underneath the pile of jumpers, the schoolbag. There's a pencil case in it too, full of pens of different colours. Some nights, when she's not faffing about online, Brit reads things to herself out of the book, the funny pages, about *realism*, the foul things people really say or tweet. She has worked out, from how the girl has positioned them on the pages, that some of the pieces have been written to go together as if they are in sort of dialogues with each other, the right wing stuff answered by a voice bigger than it, the earth speaking, or time or her favourite season, and the story about the person with no face answering the ways people are used by the technology they think they're the ones using, and the foul things people send people on twitter answered by the story of the girl who refuses the people who want her to dance herself to death.

Brit quite often gets the book out specifically to read that villager story.

But invariably she ends up feeling bad when she looks at the Hot Air book.

One reason is that at the front, under the words RISE MY DAUGHTER ABOVE, a different older handwriting has written this: *All through your life people will be ready and waiting to tell you that what you are speaking is a lot of hot air. This is because people like to put people down. But I want you to write your thoughts and ideas in this book, because then this book and what you write in it will help lift your feet off the ground and even to fly like you are a bird, since hot air rises and can not just carry us but help us rise above.*

This paragraph of handwriting really annoys Brit.

Her mother never gave or made her a book like this one.

Sometimes she thinks she could try to find the school. She could return the book in the schoolbag to the school and they will maybe have a forwarding address for it.

The girl said she had a little brother.

Brit wonders where he is too. Maybe she could find him and give him the book to give to his sister.

Vivunt spe.

Or she could just burn the book and throw the schoolbag away.

She doesn't yet know which of these she'll end up doing.

Josh texts her back a week after she texted him from that train.

It means live in hope or they are living hope. Something like that. Unusual conjugation. No doubt you already looked it up on google. Hope you're okay Brit jx. Him using her name like that at the end of the message made her feel like he was patronizing her.

She won't yet have seen Josh again, by March.

She said to Torq, the first time she was on shift with him after she got back from Scotland, that she'd been to the country he's from.

I heard, he said. I know all the latest news. Where were you exactly, Britannia?

She got up a map on her phone.

Here. Then here. Then here.

He pointed to a place on the map quite close to one of the places she'd been, and then he said something she didn't understand because he was speaking in that melted sounding language they have there.

Fàsaidh leanabh is labhraidh e faclan a theanga fhèin, faclan a dh'fhoghlamaicheas na h-uibhir den t-saoghal dha nach eil nam faclan ann. Ach, dhan leanabh 's gach fear is tè a dham bheil a dhàimh, tha brìgh sna faclan sin agus is eòl dhaibh am brìgh. Èist rium, bi an leanabh sin is greim aca, bhon fhìor-thoiseach. Air gach sian, dorch is soilleir, trom is eutrom, a thig an rathad.

For some reason just hearing it made her angry. It made her near tears. It felt like being bullied did, back when she was at school and had to pretend she wasn't clever. Then Torq made it worse by smiling at her like he really liked her while he made the impossible sounding sounds.

Her throat started to hurt like it does when you try to stop yourself crying. It was the language that was making it hurt.

What I'm saying, he said, roughly translated and losing a lot of the beauty in the translation, is this.

A child grows up saying words that the rest of the world tells the child aren't words. But the child and everybody the child holds dear all know that the words mean, and what the words mean. Listen, that child will be equipped, from the very beginning. For everything, dark and light, heavy and light, that life will bring to that child.

Whatever, Brit said. If you say so.

It's called Living Language, Torquil said. Smior na cànain. It's a poem. Written on my heart, Britannia, like Calais and Mary Queen of Scots.

I have no fucking idea what you're on about most of the time, mate, she said.

Uh huh, he said. But hey. I'm well equipped
for that.

All that Really channel Most Haunted stuff they
taught you in your childhood up there must have
deepfried your brain, she called at him down the
corridor with her throat pulsing inside her.

It was pulsing like she was a string on a musical
instrument that was being played against its will.

Different languages shouldn't be allowed in
England.

Britain. She meant Britain.

Basically, from then on she'd find herself more
often than not hanging out and signing up for shifts
with Russell.

She is sorry for the hunger striker.

But there's nothing she can do.

She picks up the bowl and gives it to one of the
kitchen deets to take to the kitchen.

End of day.

Outside the IRC the little hedges are now one
hedge. You can't see where one plant ends and
another begins.

She is down on her knees breaking the branch off
when Stel goes past.

You all right, Brit? Lost something?

Got it now, Brit says. Thanks.

This time next week it'll be lovely and light with
the hour going forward, Stel says.

Brit nods.

Yeah, lovely.

She puts her hand in her pocket with the twig inside it. On the train she crushes one of the leaves and holds to her nose the smell of the green colour.

What you doing with all that boxwood in here? her mother says next morning, when she comes in and sees the pile of twigs, dried, old, dull, green, fresh, shining, on Brit's table in her room, because Brit's still in bed so well past the alarm going off that her mother's had to come in to get her up.

Boxwood.

Who knew her mother would know what kind of a hedge it is?

Her mother never lets on about knowing anything, but she does, she knows loads.

The 24-hour BBC news is already on and blaring in the front room as per. Same old meltdown. What on earth'll happen etc. Same old noise. Same old same old, over and over, lots of noise, signifying nothing. Phrase from school. William Shakespeare. They'd read it round the class. A man takes over a kingdom by foul means not fair. But the ghosts are on to him, and the trees form an army and march to get him.

She gets up.

She pulls on clothes.

Her mother has taken the hedge twigs and put them in the kitchen bin. Brit sees them in there when she goes to put the teabag in.

Got to stop taking my work home with me, she thinks to herself.

But right now? It's still October.

There's a countrywide wintering to go through yet.

Out on the old battlefield the autumn tourists are heading between the flags marking where the different armies were.

They wander past the Well of the Dead. They take photos of the Memorial Cairn. They visit the only cottage left standing now that was there on the day of the battle.

They bend to read the low stones carved with the names of the clans that fell at this place or that, the day the Jacobite army led by Charlie the Scottish Frenchman fought the Government army led by his cousin Billy the English German in the cold spring sleet and the hail, and the soldiers of Billy's army, largely because they'd lost so badly to the Highlanders the last few times they fought, and had since worked to perfect the new sideways stabbing action with their bayonets and swords and the new kneeling/standing rifle-firing and loading rota, managed to beat them, and all the local men and women and children out counting the corpses on the road between Culloden and Inverness in the aftermath of the battle had to hide from the Redcoats so they'd not end up being bloody meat themselves.

Fastforward a blink of history's eye, 272 years from then, give or take a half year.

Here's today's battlefield:

a child runs across the grass over the bones of the dead and leaps into the arms of a young woman.

Can you imagine seeing a heart leap? That's what it looks like.

The young woman wraps her arms around the child.

They stand there like that and it's like the world can't not coalesce round it.

Then what looks like a small mob of people in uniform is running towards them across the grass. From a distance it looks like someone must be making a comedy film, like an old Keystone Cops silent, there are so many people running with such fierceness at a woman and a child.

It's not hard for the uniforms to surround them. They don't run away, the child and the woman.

They just stand there hugging as if they're one person, not two.

The people in the uniforms separate the woman and the child.

The woman and the child are taken separately back to the main car park.

The child is placed in the back of one van and the woman, who they handcuff, in the other.

The vans start up and drive off.

A few tourists who see it happening follow the woman, the child and the officials to the car park, keeping their distance. A few more people round the car park, including some actors who've come out of the visitor centre dressed up as people from the past, a bit like ghosts, ghosts from both sides of the battle, watch them being loaded into the vans.

One of the actors gets a phone out from under his costume and starts taking phone footage. Several people get their phones out to do this. When they hold the phones up people in SA4A uniforms come towards them waving their arms and shouting at them to stop filming.

The people keep filming anyway. They film the vans going.

When the vans have gone they film the white woman who is standing shouting in the middle of the road at the going vans, like shouting at them'll make a difference. They film her being loaded into the police car. They film the police car driving off with the woman in it.

They film the man watching it all, who comes over to them and asks the people who've recorded what's happening on their phones if he can have their contact details.

They ask him, what just happened? What's going on? What was it about?

Then it's back to the trail over the war graves, or into the visitor centre, warmer than out here. The 360-degree CGI re-enactment of the last battle fought on British soil is reputed to be really good, to really bring the battle to life. 700 Highlanders dead in three minutes and a free audio guide with GPS. Not too expensive, rated excellent, five stars from most of the people on TripAdvisor.

And that's all there is, for now anyway.

Story over.

Well, almost:

April.

It teaches us everything.

The coldest and nastiest days of the year can happen in April. It won't matter. It's April.

The English word for the month comes from the Roman Aprilis, the Latin aperire: to open, to uncover, to make accessible, or to remove whatever stops something from being accessible. It maybe also partly comes from the name of Aphrodite, Greek goddess of love, whose happy fickleness with various gods mirrors the month's own showery-sunny fickleness.

Month of sacrifice and month of playfulness. Month of restoration, of fertility-festivity. Month when the earth and the buds are already open, the creatures asleep for the winter have woken and are already breeding, the birds have already built their nests, birds that this time last year didn't exist, busy bringing to life the birds that'll replace them this time next year.

Spring-cuckoo month, grass-month.

In Gaelic its name means the month that fools mistake for May. April Fool's Day also probably marks what was the old end of the new year celebrations. Winter has Epiphany. Spring's gifts are different.

Month of dead deities coming back to life.

In the French revolutionary calendar, along with the last days of March, it becomes Germinal, the month of return to the source, to the seed, to the germ of things, which is maybe why Zola gave the novel he wrote about hopeless hope this revolutionary title.

April the anarchic, the final month, of spring the great connective.

Pass any flowering bush or tree and you can't not hear it, the buzz of the engine, the new life already at work in it, time's factory.

Acknowledgements and thanks

I'm indebted, above all, to the refugees and detainees who've spoken to me or written about what it's like to be detained indefinitely at a UK Immigration Removal Centre and especially to an anonymous friend who told me about everyday life in this country's IRCs.

Thank you, Simon,
thank you, Anna,
thank you, Hermione, Ellie, Lesley B, Lesley L, Sarah C and everyone at Hamish Hamilton and Penguin.

Thank you, Andrew,
thank you, Tracy,
and everyone at Wylie's.

Huge thank you to Tacita Dean.

Thank you, Julie Fowlis and Raghnaid Sandilands.

Thank you, Rachel Foss, Gerri Kimber,
· Andrea Newbery, Howard Nelson.

Special thanks to Kate Thomson and Lucy Harris.

Thank you, Mary.

Thank you, Xandra.

Thank you, Sarah.